HOSPIT

MW00974242

The Journey of Welcome

Campus Ministry at a Historically Black College

By
James G. Daniely
BA, M. Div., D. Min.

Llumina Press

Copyright © 2005 James Daniely

All rights reserved. No part of this publication may be reproduced or transmitted in any form or by any means electronic or mechanical, including photocopy, recording, or any information storage and retrieval system, without permission in writing from both the copyright owner and the publisher.

Requests for permission to make copies of any part of this work should be mailed to Permissions Department, Llumina Press, PO Box 772246, Coral Springs, FL 33077-2246

ISBN: 1-59526-001-3

Library of Congress Control Number: 2005905799

Printed in the United States of America by Llumina Press

Table of Contents

Acknowledgments

My heartfelt gratitude is extended to several friends and supporters who helped me to create and finish this project:

The late Eve-Lyn Dayton Gulledge who worked as the Office Assistant for United Campus Ministry during the described period and who provided continuity during my absences to study at Union Theological Seminary;

Mrs. Victoria Jackson Gray Adams, the Queen Mother, who prayed for this ministry before it became a reality and who mentored, nurtured, and advised this preacher in numerous ways that have positively affected this preacher and this ministry;

My students, who trusted me, shared with me, and formed the laboratory of this experience beginning in 1998 and continuing to this day;

Dr. Charles Brown for guiding me through this process and critiquing it every step of the way. Finally, I praise God for allowing me this place in time and calling me to this work as I learned to embrace the mission of Hospitality.

I.

THESIS STATEMENT

The transition from home to college represents the loss of a safe and sacred place for the developing college student. This is quite a significant loss of "home space" in which to become fully oneself. Also inclusive is the loss of "sacred space" in which to appropriate and participate in the redemptive activity of God in Christ. The combined loss creates a fracture, not only in personal space, but also in a person's sense of self and in his/her perception that there is "a faithfulness at the heart of things."

In this instance, the world of college or university becomes an inhospitable and unreal place. Here, hospitality is defined as hospes, or safe space, where the real self has a guardian both individually, in the person of the Campus Minister, and communally, in the campus fellowship. Since the deepest human need is to be in touch with a safe reality (including the ultimate reality of God), appropriate pastoral care can re-establish broken connections within the self and encourage the growth of a new, fuller self in the formative community of believers.

When church and society does not care for young pilgrims engaged in this transition, it abuses them by minimizing their pain and thwarting their development as future leaders. Their pain is significant, because this college transition can be experienced as a psychic/spiritual death where discontinuity replaces continuity, stasis stymies growth, and separation destroys connection. Such pain has a deep spiritual dimension as well, in that such a crisis of dislocation calls into radical question the hospitality of God's creation. For psychic and spiritual health to be restored, hospitality must be restored. This is the goal of my project: the restoration of hospitality through intentional pastoral care, where healing, sustaining, guiding and reconciling ministry seeks to restore safe and hospitable space on campus for later adolescents in crisis.

II.

METHOD

The method is qualitative and transformational. No empirical tests will be administered. Case studies (the bedrock of pastoral care since Anton Boisen) will be offered. These case studies are not meant to be large enough to constitute a quantitative study; thus, their purpose is suggestive and heuristic. The author sincerely hopes that those interested in statistical analysis will perform their own studies based on initial intuitions. The purpose of this study is ethnographic; that is, descriptive and directed toward the goal of restoring psychic and spiritual well-being.

III.

VERIFICATION PRINCIPLE

The verification of my thesis and method will be in the restoration of a sense of continuity, integrity, growth and connection with self, others, and God, in those seeking pastoral care. Also, it is expected that as the student becomes re-attached to safety and reality in the care of the minister and the fellowship, he/she will cherish his/her uniqueness; accept his/her insignificance; live with his/her capacity for un-integration; be receptive and open, and know how to make use of the world without needing to react to it; find and contribute to the inherited cultural tradition; and tolerate essential isolation without fleeing to false relationships or retreating into deleterious insulation.

CHAPTER 1

"Father, forgive them, for they know not what they do."
(NKJ)

Students come to college somewhat alone, frightened, and often ill-equipped for the pressures that await them. They are meeting new people, making new friends and experiencing a sense of freedom that is for some very stressful. They need something familiar and accepting. When they come to Chapel or Bible Study, they are looking for an expression with which they are at least familiar. If they are also made to feel at home then they will return, and some will stay awhile. For others, the sense of loss is too great and they return home before the semester is over. Yet still for some the sense of loss and loneliness creates a perilous set of circumstances that often lead to acting out in ways that are detrimental to their total development.

Our setting is a small town across the Appomattox River from Petersburg, Virginia. Although in Chesterfield County, Virginia State University resembles a small island inhabited by some 2,300 resident students. They share the facilities with another 2,300 commuting students.[1] To complete the dynamics of interactions, we must add to this mix another 400 visitors that include faculty, administrators, staff, and contractual workers. The primary Campus is nestled on about one hundred and forty acres, high above and overlooking the Appomattox River.

---

[1] Virginia State University enrollment office records a steady increase in enrollment since the late 1980's. By 2002, the undergraduate enrollment peaked at 4,600 students, with more than 55 percent females and 97 percent African American.

The University was founded in 1882 at its present location and serves primarily the African-American Community. As to distinction, it is the first 'land grant institution for higher education' in the nation. Recently, the General Assembly has agreed to fully subsidize that status in direct response to Governor Gilmore.

Our context is the United Campus Ministry at Virginia State University. It is an ecumenical ministry, established in 1989 by the Virginia Annual Conference of the United Methodist Church and the Presbyterian Church, U.S.A.

The ministry began with a part-time person, Mrs. Victoria Jackson Gray Adams, functioning without a facility on campus or a connection for legitimacy. As a layperson, she was appointed to what was part-time work, and labored for many years in an attempt to initiate and sustain contact with the students, staff and faculty. Those were trying years in many respects. Yet, her clarity in articulating the vision for the ministry, as well as her prayers and tenacity in seeing the task to a conclusion, were invaluable. Therefore, undergirding the successes we have experienced is, I believe, a correlation of her urging of the Lord and her adamant stance that the ministry would succeed.

Over the last four years, we were housed in several different locations prior to our settlement within the Student Union building. Is it coincidental that once a permanent location was settled upon, the ministry began to grow? No, of course not! However, there are other dynamics that I wish to explore before making any lasting judgments about the reasons for our success.

Finally, the context of ministry would be incomplete without mentioning the University's support of what we do. The administration, under President Eddie N. Moore, has allocated us space, telephone services, computers and the technological support to maintain them. They have been our quiet allies and truly, without their support, we would not be here. In return for these considerations I offer counseling services to the entire student body, participate in the Opening Convocation and officiate at Founder's Day and the Commencement Services.

At present, my role is to give a voice to the practice of hospitality and interpret its significance. With a total of approximately seven people, we serve the other students and talk with them. These same seven also lead us in worship. After the service, a small group surrounds me, waiting to greet me personally and comment on the service. This is my opportunity to suggest that they spend a few moments discussing their comments with their peers. Else, their small talk is not about the sermon but about current issues of significance to them. Sometimes, I deliberately move to a particular area of the Chapel to be near specific persons who have been with the ministry awhile to help them in shaping a group. Our goal is for the students to initiate and sustain this practice. Nevertheless, I walk the room and speak to people while they are snacking, attempting to bring others into the conversation. The underlying reality is that many people leave before we have a chance to engage them. On an average, we interact with about half of those attending, and only a half of that group intimately. Our students have initiated conversations about music and choir formations for the service, so I do not want to suggest that their leadership has been absent. What I am searching for is a vehicle to transform us, as well as our worship, into agents of hospitality. The added dimension might be the students' ownership of the entire worship experience.

Beyond the group worship experience, I view hospitality as the offering of a safe place for persons to come and just "hang out." It encompasses a space where conversations are open without quick judgments or censure of thought. This involves, but is not limited to, extended office hours, an assortment of snacks and a warm, embracing presence in the office. Lyn Gulledge and I were willing to embrace the students and grew to a comfortable diligence in welcoming all, allowing them the time and opportunity to get to know and accept us. Many times just being available to them, without an appointment or an agenda, was the difference that accelerated the growth and development of the richness of our fellowship.

The theology involved is the incarnation of Christ. Often, I am caught off guard by the deliberateness of that image. I am also struck by the allusion that I become the Christ for them at those moments. That is a scary thought and one that I have never articulated. However, it is exhilarating to understand that Christ is empowering and energizing what we do. This language is included at the sharing of the Sacrament of the Lord's Supper, but I am not conscious of using it anywhere else. Perhaps, unconsciously, that is the underlying tenet to what is occurring. There are moments of tremendous beauty and ministry as students and I interact under the felt influence of the Holy Spirit. It was not always that way. In fact, we need to go back to 1998 and walk together through some of the defining moments of this ministry as we tried to discern through learning experiences what God was trying to do with us, for us, and through us. How did I give voice to the practice of hospitality and interpret its significance? What was the understanding gained by participants in the worship service that allowed them to move from casual observer to active participant? What did they experience or sense as they came into the office that indicated this was a safe place? What are the ingredients or dynamics of a hospitable place?

Fall 1998

In 1998 I was beginning my twentieth year of ministry and was newly appointed by the United Methodist Church to be the Campus Minister. As an ordained Baptist Minister in an ecumenical setting, I was stretched and called to respond instinctually in those situations where I felt incomplete. Ultimately, the students would provide the stimulus for shaping, questioning and articulating my present positions. Walk with us as the journey unfolds. I begin this story with our first Bible study.

Bible Study: September 9, 1998

I have placed flyers all over Campus inviting students to the Bible study. Will they come? As I nervously wait for the appointed time, I set chairs in a circle and hope. One student comes in and looks around. It is 7:05. I smile and welcome him. Seeing no one else, he asks: "What time is the Bible study?" I say, "We begin at 7:30, but please have a seat and fill out this card." He says he will come back and goes out the door. At 7:25 two young ladies come in and sit. I introduce myself and hand out the blank information cards. They take them without hesitating. Immediately, several others come in. I am standing in a room with seven young ladies who are busy filling out the information cards, wondering, "Where are the brothers?" By 7:45, we have finished brief introductions, bonded at some levels and I realize that I have not prepared for the study! What will I do? Without missing a beat, I ask them to open their Bibles and turn to their favorite scripture. (Of those gathered, five walked in with their Bibles). As each student read their particular passage, I asked the following questions: Why did you choose that passage? What does it mean to you? Is there anyone who wants to add something else to the discussion? Participation from the group was going very well. I teased them gently and affirmed their understanding of what was being said. When the room became quiet, I would get nervous and begin to ramble. My last questions to them went something like this: What does this passage reveal about your present relationship with Christ? Does it assure you that you are on target, or does it urge you to change your outlook? Finally, nine o'clock arrived and I announced the close of our session. I invited them to worship on Sunday and encouraged them to bring their roommates. We had prayer and I said goodnight. No one moved! Ok, what's going on? They noticed the look on my face and someone said, "Rev, we need to talk some more. This is the best Bible study I have ever been to, and I don't want to leave." I was amazed! We were forming a bond simply because they were allowed a voice. I had listened to their comments without judgment. In addition, they had been permitted the freedom to disagree about the possible meaning of a passage and loved it. The 'non-structure' of the structured time together was a winner in their minds.

Upon reflection, I recognize they were using literal interpretations of the Bible in their points of view, yet it did not matter. I was so grateful that they came that I was not overly concerned with their theological perspective. That would soon change as I listened to their stories, felt and understood their pain, and asked God to allow me to be a guide in their faith development. Those days were filled with anxious moments as I scrambled to meet the challenges presented to me. For example, I was being asked to counsel these young adults, a task for which I was untrained. At best, I could provide limited pastoral care. I recognized this limitation and began a search for resources to equip myself for this task, ultimately leading me to Union PSCE. Until that moment arrived, I hoped not to cause harm, while confident that God would equip me in the process.

The next opportunity to examine our journey is a sermon delivered after approximately one month with the students. In the African American experience, I believe, along with Dr. Henry Mitchell, that there are core beliefs operating at some level of consciousness. These beliefs function as a rudder in our lives to fill us with hope. One of these core beliefs is that God will provide "a way out of no way." I learned this from my great grandmother, who could barely read or write but could quote chapter and verse from the Bible. She had experienced God in such a way there was no doubt about God's ability to deliver her in times of trouble and trials. In his work, Soul Theology: The Heart of American Black Culture, Dr. Mitchell states, "...people who grow up in the Black community are spontaneously equipped with a system of core beliefs."

Sermon: September 13, 1998
Psalm 22:1-8; Luke 24:1-7   Title: "It's A New Day"

As these sisters approach the cemetery where Jesus had been laid, their outward expression was one of gloom. Their hope that this was the One had been dashed. A little more than three days ago, their spirits were high because they had found someone who treated them with respect; someone who treated them as valuable persons, not objects of service or sex. They had found someone who proclaimed 'liberty to the captives, sight to the blind,' and that all persons were accepted as equals before God. This One, Jesus of Nazareth, had made them feel special, somehow made their steps lighter, and helped them rediscover the laughter of life. But now, all was lost! They came to the place of death to prepare his body for eternal rest. They came to this place of disappointment, expecting to drown in their mutual sorrow. But wouldn't you know it? Someone, they believe, is playing a joke on them. They cannot find the body. Can you see their sorrow and frustration increasing? Can you see their sorrow turning into anger?

But wait a minute! Who are these two beings standing there, shining brighter than the morning sun? Suddenly, anger is dissipating into fear. Frustration is obliterated, and wonder is manifested. They are puzzled and filled with awe. They begin to wonder, "Could it really be true?" Their faith is quickened with the question: "Why do you look for the living among the dead?" Or in my paraphrase, "Why are you expecting the same old, same old?" It's a new day!

You see, they came expecting all the old axioms to still be in effect. They expected disappointment to remain unchanged. They expected finality to remain unchanged. In essence, they expected dead folk to remain dead! So it was then, and so it is now.

Most of us show up at our designated place, at the designated time, expecting the same ole stuff. There may be a wish that something different will occur, but there is no expectancy. We don't anticipate that God is doing something different, so we come with all of our old baggage. Those old hurts still define us. Our old assumptions still hold us captive. Those old labels are still limiting us; but it's a new day! Just like those sisters at the graveyard, we don't take to heart the full implications of the Resurrection of Jesus Christ. When God called Jesus forth from among the dead, God was indicating that new possibilities were on the horizon.

For these women, the immediate Good News was that they were not limited by their understanding of reality. In their reality, they were considered unequal to men, treated like second-class citizens, unable to fend for themselves in a male-oriented, male-dominated world. Yet God was saying, "Before any man sees it, I am revealing something marvelous to you." Hence they were able to herald this news, the Good News that Jesus lives, even to the disciples! This is a new order, not because of anything they had accomplished, but because of what God was doing. In a sense, the last would be first, and the first would be last to see it. A new day was unfolding and they were participants in the action.

Walk with me a little further. This word also implies that there is an adverse situation we too must face, which will appear to be insurmountable—something that is on the surface, an impossibility for us to overcome. Yes, you too must face your moment of crisis. I cannot tell you what your personal crisis will be, only that it is coming. It's like a freight training pulling up a mountain pass, slowly chugging and straining; but it will get there! It's coming to refine, strengthen, and prove you! Yes, it is coming. So don't try to hide from it, for it will find you! There is no profit in running from it. It will be there when you tire of running. Therefore, I suggest that you do something radical: embrace it! Yes, you heard me correctly. I said, "Embrace it!" Your moment of crisis is also your refining moment. In order for the larva to become a butterfly, it must first be wrapped in a cocoon, a sort of entombment. Without the life-giving experience of the entombment, the butterfly would not exist! What appears to be certain death becomes the reality that releases you into life.

Then the Good News is that when you go through your midnight of despair, when you feel like God has abandoned you and you are all alone, know that God is there for you. God will not leave you nor forsake you. Furthermore, when you come through your despair—and you will come through it—remember that God promised it would be that way. Now you may ask, "Rev, when did God make that promise?" My answer is, "When Jesus was raised from the dead, new possibilities were unleashed unto the world. The envelope was pushed out and now, all things are possible for the believer." Whatever you thought was impossible in your life, God says think again. Just because no member of your family has ever graduated from college does not mean that you won't. It's a new day! Just because all the girls from your high school senior class are now pregnant does not mean it has to follow you like a curse. Just because alcoholism runs in your family does not mean that you also will become an alcoholic. It's a new day! You are not a hopeless captive. God has new possibilities available to you. Will you embrace this new expectancy or will you settle for the status quo? The choice is yours. It's a new day, become new with it. Amen.

As I re-read this message, I have a profound appreciation for what was happening then. At some level of consciousness, I was claiming something for them in this sermon that I was not able to articulate personally to the group. In addition, perhaps I was anticipating developments that would later unfold. To put it another way, I was claiming an authority they had not yet given to me. Remembering my own young adult years, I was also projecting some of my issues on them. At this point, however, this was unfounded, although it came to light later that I was very much on point. In fact, the following week during our Bible study, I was asked about my ability to convincingly address, issues in their lives they had not yet shared with me. I gave the knee-jerk response:, "Oh, the Lord moves in mysterious ways." In actuality, humanity ages but does not change very much. The issues facing young adults, in most instances, although buried in different language, tend to be very similar in nature.

Young Adults and Sexuality

According to Kelly Brown Douglas, the Black church has been silent on matters of sexuality. While sexuality is about more than what we do with our genitals, it is not synonymous with sex. I believe for us the working definition will entail our self-understanding and our way of relating to the world as women and men. This segment is enriched by my reading of Sexuality and the Black Church: A Womanist Perspective by Kelly Brown Douglas and What the Bible Really Says About Homosexuality by Daniel Herminie.[2] Very early in our fellowship, the issue of sexuality and how to handle our strong desires for intimacy in responsible ways was thrust upon us. The issue was brought to the forefront by 'an unexpected pregnancy' and the subsequent marriage of a very young couple. When I was consulted, I marveled at the naïveté of the young people as the young man sought counsel. The following is real; the names have been changed to protect their confidentiality.

James and Mary

James and Mary had been high school sweethearts. They migrated from Maryland to attend college together. James was a licensed minister, a Southern Baptist and had been speaking publicly in many venues for many years. As such, he was a confident, articulate and gifted orator who had girls swooning over him. In our group gatherings, they had bragged about their practice of celibacy and openly challenged others to follow this lifestyle. In addition, they had both spoken of their goals in life, which included graduate school. James had a very out go-

---

[2] These works helped to inform me and correct me over time as I wrestled with the little I knew of the students and their histories. In self-disclosing, they left much out, leaving me to attempt pastoral care without adequate information.

ing personality, often attempting to dominate the sessions. Some of the students began deferring to his opinion. I noticed this and began to intentionally call on others for their comments, often limiting his participation to the close of sessions. Mary, on the other hand, was very shy and appeared content to bask in James' glory. Therefore, when he walked into my office with a forlorn countenance, I was unprepared for the conversation. "Doc," he blurted out, "Mary is pregnant!" Mary had not had a cycle for several months and believed she was pregnant. I sat back and did a mental inventory of what I knew of him. His father was a Pastor in Baltimore and his mother was presently in Seminary. I assumed he would be pressured to get married, but I did not share this. I gently probed him to get a sense of his thoughts. "How do you feel about Mary? What do the two of you consider to be your options?" He said he felt trapped and did not want to get married. We danced around their alleged vows of celibacy, the questions of love and commitment, the call of God on his life, and responsible behavior.

Eventually, we came back to their choices and the consequences. He was adamant about not getting married because of the pregnancy, and was very angry with Mary for doing this to him! I reminded him that he too had a responsibility to prevent an unwanted pregnancy and that he could not blame someone else for his carelessness. In addition, I told him about an adoption agency in Richmond and abortion clinics in the area. I asked him to seek his father's counsel. He informed me that his father and mother had told him not to marry this girl and that he was aware of the options I laid out for him.

Mary stopped attending the Wednesday gathering and James cut back his attendance, and every so often I would see him near the cafeteria with different sisters on his arm. When I confronted him, he told me to chill out and mind my business. After that, he stopped attending the fellowship. However, during the Thanksgiving break, I received an invitation to a wedding at his father's church! I did not attend but sent a note of congratulations and a gift for the couple. The marriage soured over a period of three years. The initial pregnancy produced twins, and then within a year, another child was born. They are now separated. James joined the military, left Mary in this area, and does not communicate with either of us. Interestingly enough, Mary returned to school and to the fellowship.

Class: Human Sexuality

Buoyed by the reality of the naivety of the students in the fellowship, I ventured 'where angels dare to go.' Beginning in the fall of 1999, I offered six sessions on human sexuality. The women were very receptive, but not the young men! In all honesty, my comments heavily supported females, depicting the young men in an unfavorable light. I suspect that once again I was projecting my own promiscuity during my adolescent years. Very often the women used these sessions to vent their frustrations at the lack of commitment among the young men of VSU. Even though my bias was evident, I also chided the women about their promiscuity. It did not help that at about this time, a common slang was being used widely on Campus. The men were affectionately referring to themselves as 'dog.' This unfortunate choice of words, fueled by several rap artists, had a negative effect on our sessions. While the brothers were affectionately calling each other 'dog,' the sisters had something else in mind when they addressed the young men in the same fashion. The young men were acting like animals in heat, mating with any available female. In this scenario, language was being used to malign the character of the innocent while accurately describing the actions and intentions of others. Ultimately, we had to curtail these sessions to seek means of healing the obvious breach that was developing.

Could I have better assessed the needs of the group and moved more quickly? Should I have anticipated the actions of James and Mary and tried to intervene? What strategies should I have put into place to support them once they announced to the world their intention to be celibate? What support could I have offered once they were married? Was my failure also their failure? I wrestle with these questions and others as I reflect on our time together.

It was my intent to bring to consciousness the power of their sexuality. I am convinced that many persons were helped by these sessions as they watched Mary's pain unfold before them. In fact, several told me much later that Mary's sharing helped them to deal with their pain. I hoped that our openness with a taboo subject allowed young adults to honestly evaluate their sexuality and not be ashamed of it. Our interactions were honest and facilitated our faith journey. We explored issues together and I allowed them to make their own choices, even when I thought their decisions were poor. This scripture was selected to name the chapter because in many instances, I was oblivious to the outcome of our interactions. We walked together, learned together, were wounded together, and somehow came through whole. "Father, forgive them, for they know not what they do."

CHAPTER 2

Love & Grace: Experiential Theology in Action

Love and grace are the two theological concepts that define our ministry of hospitality. Theologically, love is construed as God's benevolent concern for humankind and humanity's response to it. Grace is the unmerited love and favor of God toward humans and the special virtue given to a person by God. It is my contention that we receive 'abundant grace' in all of our interactions with each other, else great damage could occur. In the laboratory of life, we are only able to use what gifts we have: to meet persons at the point they are with love, help in the healing process and hope that we do not hinder the process. I have invited these persons to walk in love and grace as they deal with the issues of life through faith. As we attempt to model love and grace, it is imperative that we look at the methods cited in the biblical record as our primary models. Since a great percentage of my time is spent talking with troubled persons, my guide is the image of Jesus as liberator and fulfiller of life.

In this segment, the works of Leroy T. Howe and James E. Loder[3] are used extensively as a corrective. I use verbatim interviews with students who have walked with us for at least two

---

[3] Howe, Leroy T. *The Image of God: A Theology for Pastoral Care & Counseling.* *Nashville:* Abingdon Press, 1995.

Loder, James E. *The Logic of the Spirit: Human Development in the Theological Perspective.* San Francisco: Jossey-Bass Publishers, 1998.

years. These are actual incidents presented to me, the counsel given, and sermons delivered as reinforcement tools. The persons have been disguised, but the issues are not.

Verbatim: M.A.

M.A. is a graduating senior from Philadelphia who is in love with T from New York. She has been active in our fellowship for three years. She was adopted and never knew her birth parents. During her freshman year, she received a call from her "mom" saying her birth mother had contacted them and wanted to meet her. Amidst the excitement of the potential meeting, the mother became ill and ultimately died before the reunion with her daughter. At the funeral, MA is seated with her natural family and is received as one of them. After the service, her sisters mentioned her amazing resemblance to their mother, and explained that their mother had struggled with drug addiction and that was the primary reason that she gave up her baby for adoption. MA's struggles and her feelings of rejection all centered on her inability to form lasting relationships.

MA: I can't believe what I am going through right now! I don't know what I am feeling about my birth mother. My sense of loss is not what I expected. My major is pissing me off. My boyfriend is acting like a jerk. What am I to do?

JD: What do you mean? Do about what?

MA: I mean, I am supposed to feel hurt, right? Well, I feel hurt all right, but not about her death. I am hurt that she would just give me up! I would never give up my child. I am sorry but that's not right!

JD: I can understand your feelings somewhat. But let's look a moment from her possible position. Maybe she was thinking about you more than you are giving her credit for. Maybe she thought that giving you up was the right thing to do under the circumstances. (Pause) How is your relationship with your adopted family?

MA: We are cool and all that. I mean, my mother loves me to death. But she is all in my business all the time!

JD: Do you understand that as being nosy or as being concerned for you?

MA: I am not feeling that right now. All I feel is that I can't breathe!

JD: What do you mean?

MA: Well, I want to go to the beach this weekend with my boyfriend and she is all up in that!

JD: Do you think that is a wise thing to do at this point in your life...in the relationship?

MA: (Long pause) "Well, you see, I just got to know."

JD: What is it that "you got to know"?

MA: I just got to know if that's all he wants? If that's the case, he's history!

JD: I assume by that you mean if he wants you sexually?

MA: Yes! If all he wants is that, then he is not worthy of my affection. If that's the case, he's just like the rest of them.

JD: I feel you. But do you feel it is a wise thing to go away for the weekend with him? What possible signal are you sending? If your intentions are not to become intimate with him, then why put yourself in that predicament?

MA: You make it sound like I am being dishonest. Can't people just go away for the weekend without sex being in the picture?

JD: Yes, of course they can. But they lay out the ground rules beforehand and all parties are on the same page. You sound as if this is a test for him and that he does not know that sex is not a part of the agenda for the weekend. If that's the game you are playing, then you need to inform him of your true intentions. Women have been raped under similar circumstances when young men, or older men for that matter, perceive that they are being played with. That's a dangerous game you are playing! I suggest you re-think this whole scenario before you get in too deep! And yes, it is dishonest.

MA: (Long Pause) He would never do that to me! He knows that I love him and he would not do anything to hurt me!

JD: Oh, please define love for me.

MA: Oh, come on Rev, you know what I mean!

JD: Do I know what you mean? Help me out and explain it like I am from Mars.

MA: OK! I feel you. I remember we went through the book: Men are from Mars, Women are from Venus The point was that men understand the same sentences differently than women and that we send mixed signals, right?

JD: Exactly! You are sending a potentially dangerous message here and I want you to recognize it and decide what you are going to do about it. Not only that, you have been with me three years and you seem to forget the things we said about what love is and what it is not! Or are the definitions for the class and not for life?

MA: No, the lessons are not just for the class. But this is my life and I need to know if he is the one!

JD: Ok, I understand your desire to know if his intentions are good. Yet, to put yourself in this risky position is not a good idea. Not only that, but common sense should tell you not to put yourself in a situation where you can be tempted. If you love yourself, not to mention the young man, I advise you not to do this.

MA: All right. You sound like my mother.

JD: Well, good. I hope one of us gets through to you.

(MA goes ahead with her plans for the weekend and is greatly disappointed with the outcome. True to form, the young man expects sex as the treat for weekend and she does not oblige. She returns broken and hurt over his lack of sensitivity to her desires for her life.)

MA: Hey Rev. What's up?

JD: What's up with you?

MA: You were right. I was wrong, end of subject.

JD: Hold on. What are we talking about? (I had heard from another sister in the fellowship how things had gone down and that she was devastated. I had not seen her for almost two weeks.)

MA: About T. All he wanted was sex. I was so hurt!

JD: I am so sorry. How did you come to that conclusion?

MA: We went away and he was all over me! I never would have thought he was like that.

JD: Like what? Like a human being away for the weekend with the one he loves, is that what you mean?

MA: Oh, you funny. You know what I mean.

JD: MA, not many people could pass that test! Did you not know he would be interested in you sexually? Wake up.

MA: Am I wrong to want time alone without the sex?

JD: No, my daughter. It's just not realistic to expect someone to read your mind. Did you share your expectations for the weekend? And even if you made it absolutely clear that you expect to be a virgin when you get married, being there for the weekend was sending mixed signals!

MA: Well, I did not tell him we were not going to have sex, but I did tell him I was going to have sex only with my husband.

JD: Those are fairly clear statements, but the journey to the beach with him alone was not good judgment. I still insist that it sent the wrong message. So, what now?

MA: Well, I have given up on men. I guess I'll be an old maid!

In looking at MA, I have identified the issue of intimacy as a dominant factor in her life. Together with the sense of abandonment, she has struggled to develop trust in anyone other than her adopted mother. Even with her, there is a sense of an underlying distrust. What I am most concerned about, however, are her games of intimacy and isolation. While I applaud her stance of virginity, I am concerned that it is not a real concern with morality but with commitment. My stance arises because this is the third occurrence, to my knowledge, where she has placed herself in harm's way to eliminate a potential suitor. Here, the grace of God is so evident that it drips from this young lady. So many young ladies have been raped in similar circumstances. The incidence of date rape is on the increase in all the statistics coming our way from around the nation. God's providential care overrode her stupidity for being so naïve to put herself in that dangerous position. At any rate, I am lost on how to get to the root of the issue.

Verbatim: DD

DD is a referral from one of the faculty members. He is a twenty-five year old male struggling with issues of homosexuality. Although he denies this is his sexual preference, he is presently rooming with an older adult who has raped him several times (?) without a police report being filed. When he comes to me, it is for assistance in getting transportation to travel to and from school. He has been in the military but his benefits have not kicked in yet. Meanwhile, he's at the mercy of friends and acquaintances. He discloses that has not eaten in several days because his meal card has been stolen/lost. There is a $25 fee to replace this and I agree to help him with that so that possibly, he can relax and formulate a plan of action. We walk over to Food Services and take care of the matter. While there, we decide to get a bite to eat. He asks if I would sit with him and we begin to share. Due to the similarity in initials, I will be "Rev." in this verbatim.

DD: I really want to thank you for hooking me up like this. Can we sit over by the window? Dr. H. said you were ok and that I could trust you.

Rev: You are welcome.

DD: I have been walking to and from school for about three weeks since I quit my job.

Rev: What happened that would have made you quit your job?

DD: You see, I got beat up after work. They broke my jaw...(voice trails off) And I wanted to put all my focus on my schoolwork. And besides, when my benefits start coming in, all will be cool. I am supposed to get a little disability from the Army plus my GI Bill! (Very excitedly)

Rev: So, now you just are waiting for the checks, right?

DD: Yeah. But the VA office on Campus was late in sending in my paperwork and that puts me behind, so I was working to try to make ends meet.

Rev: So tell me, what are you studying and how are you doing?

DD: I want to be an engineer but I am behind and my professors won't cut me any slack. They seem to think I always have an excuse for everything and they are not very sympathetic to my situation.

Rev: Well, do you?

DD: I know to them it may seem like that, but a lot has been going on this semester. I have to get back and forth to Richmond for the VA Hospital to fix my jaw, I am involved with the Victim/Witness Assistance program, dealing with Social Services, the District 19 Mental Health program, and trying to find a place to live closer to VSU.

Rev: (I am thinking to myself, "Damn, that's a load!") My, my, my.

DD: You think that's a lot too, don't you? But my professors don't give an inch. They won't let me make up assignments or anything.

Rev: Have you documents to prove what's been happening to you?

DD: Well, yes and no. I have the police report for the assault and a doctor's note from the VA for my surgery to repair my jaw. The Veteran Affair's office has been trying to cover my back, but they don't have any pull with the professors. I haven't been able to keep the other appointments because I don't have transportation. Walking everywhere is hard.

Rev: So how do you go about setting priorities?

DD: Well, school is first. But I have to walk for an hour to get here and that backpack must weigh 50 pounds. So most days I am late, especially when my legs are hurting.

Rev: What's next?

DD: I have been praying to God to help me and to take control of my life so I can get it together.

Rev: That may not be the solution to your problems. My mother always told me: "Boy, the Lord won't do for you what you can do for yourself." She wanted me to take the initiative and then ask God to boost my effort.

DD: I see what you mean. But, Rev, it is hard trying to do all the stuff I need to do.

Rev: Yes, it can be hard. Where is your family? Are they able to lend a hand?

DD: Rev, I don't have a family I like talking about. I was adopted and my mom put me out when I turned 18. I have been on my own ever since. My grandmother tries to help but she needs more than she has just to take care of herself. I must handle this on my own.

Rev: What would you like for me to do?

DD: Look, you have done a lot by getting me this meal card. I can eat now. If I can just find a place to live that is closer to Campus, I will be all right.

Rev: Where have you looked so far?

DD: That's the problem. Since my checks are not coming in yet, I don't have the money to put a deposit down on a room or something. It's a catch 22! I am damned if I do and damned if I don't!

Rev: So how are you able to stay where you are if you don't have an income?

DD: Well, it's not like I want to be there, but it's all I have. He's a member of my church and he said I could stay there until I got it together. You know, he came on to me once or twice but I explained to him that I was not like that. I mean, I have done it before, but I am not like that. I had to do something, you know. After he raped me, I went down to the Men's shelter, but I could only stay there at night and then for only eight days. Man, I got to live somewhere so I went back to live with him. (Voice trailed off and tears began to run down his face)

Rev: I am so sorry, brother.

DD: I told him we could not be hanging out like that and he said he'd be cool with me.

Rev: What exactly does that mean?

DD: It means we will not be together like that unless I consent and I will not consent.

Rev: I hope you are right. Yet, my fear is that since he's attacked you before and no charges were filed, he will do it again. The fact that you are living with him without any visible means of support might lead him, and others, to believe that you like being his lover.

DD: But Rev, its not like that! But where else can I go? It's not like I have all these options, you know. Maybe if you would intervene on my behalf instead of accusing me of something I am not about... (Gets up from the table and walks away angrily)

Is DD in denial about his sexual preference? Or is he just a young man going through a difficult period, trying to find his way? In talking with his Veteran's Affairs representative, it is confirmed that he's had an ongoing battle with depression and mental health issues. I will refer him to a competent professional. In addition, there is a history of sexual abuse in his life and the assault was related to sexual favors. Grace is demonstrated in his life daily by the general kindness that strangers offer him. He is a very likeable fellow with a quick mind. However, there is a darkness that pervades him and as I see him walking around Campus, he is always alone. He is continually in my prayers. With these two, DD & MA, uppermost in my mind, I begin my sermon preparation. (I made some calls on DD's behalf and was received warmly. I disclosed none of his personal issues but did share that many verifiable factors were affecting his productivity. I asked for grace wherever possible and for an opportunity for him to do extra work in lieu of makeup work. Two professors said they would assent to that if he asked for it. Two others reminded me that the student has the opportunity to drop the class up until the week of finals if necessary. Although helpful information, this option is not profitable for someone on any type of assistance dependent upon a full load of courses.)

As my week ends, I am searching for a word that heals, while listening to MA and DD in my mind. Calamitous circumstances are unfolding elsewhere that will harshly impact our week. The sermon for the week:

"What God Has For You"
Deuteronomy 30: 11 ff

Sunday, September 9, 2001

It is a popular saying or understanding in today's culture that this is a given. So many copies of the song were sold that everyone just assumed this must be a fact. After all, it was the Gospel radio station playing this song, so it must be right. Then we heard many preachers begin to expound very eloquently on the matter and it was a forgone conclusion: What God has for me, is for me. The idea behind this song appeared to be that if God wanted you to have something, it was a done deal. That sounds good, but what does the Bible say about this idea? "What you mean preacher? They said it on the radio, and they sang the song. What is left to do but accept it?" Well, the problem is that the basis of my faith is not the radio, nor the songs being sung, or even what some famous preacher says! My faith is based ultimately on the Jesus revealed in the Bible and the Triune God working in and through the Bible and the world. So today, I want us to reason together. In fact, I want us to do more than reason together; I want us to put away this lie of the enemy forever. Are you walking with me?

The scripture before us today is an excellent point to begin. Beginning with verse eleven, let us read again: "For this commandment which I command you today, it is not too mysterious for you, nor is it far off." What is a commandment? Is it something that, as followers of the Most High, we can debate about? NO! What is it then? It is a word to obey; that is, if you want the full benefit of your relationship with God. You see, there are benefits to being right with God! Ok. That is the understanding required before going on any further. Therefore God, through Moses in this instance, tells us that this is not some great mystery for you. In other words, what I am asking of you is not weird or strange or foreign to you. Neither is it far from you.

Well, God, if this thing is not far from me, where is it? Before God tells us where it is, there is a word about where it is not! First, it is not in heaven. There is no need to send an emissary to heaven to receive this word. Neither is this word beyond the sea. No need to send someone to get it and bring it back. So it is not out there someplace. Ok, Lord, where is it? It is very near, in your mouth and in your heart. Oh my, if it is that close, what is the problem? The problem is not that we don't know this word.

The problem, my friends, lies somewhere else. The matter before us, the 'something' for us to do, is to obey the word. That, my brothers and sisters, is the real issue. After we have this word, we must obey it. It is set before us as life and good, or death and evil.

"Now, come on, preacher, why would anyone choose death and evil over life and good?" I am glad you asked that question, because I do not know. What I do know is that it happens all too often.

Let us first look at what is equal to life and good. Moses says to the people, and to you and me, to love God and walk in His ways is to choose life! Well, what is in it for me if I chose this pattern of life? To live, multiply and be blessed. "Wait a minute, preacher! I thought you said what God has for me is for me. Was that a lie?" No, what I said was that the popular understanding of it is a lie. If you love the Lord and follow His commandments, keep His statutes and His judgments, then what God has for you, is for you. God will not deny good things to those who love Him; but the proof of that love is obedience! That is the part that is not talked about. Some folks make it seem like all you have to do is believe God is for you, and everything under the sun will fall in your lap. That is the lie! The benefits flow from obedience, not knowledge alone. If it were just knowledge, Satan would be the 'bomb!' He knows all of the commandments of God, but he does not follow them.

So if you want the benefits, you must walk the walk. The promises of God cover all aspects of your life: long life, a fruitful life and a blessed life. What more could you possibly want? This is the place to be. As a child of God, God wants you to be blessed and to live a fruitful and long life. God wants everything you touch to be blessed. God wants you to have means, so that you can be a blessing to someone else. God wants you to be anointed and powerful in the Spirit, so that when you pray, you can lay hands on the sick and they will recover. God wants you to be wise so that when others come to you, you can give them godly counsel. God wants you to be plentiful so that your children and your children's children down through the generations will have the opportunity to hear of the goodness of God. Therefore, what God has for you, is for you, if you obey the God of your salvation.

However, the flip side of the issue is the curse of disobedience. Hear the word: "But if your heart turns away so that you do not hear and are drawn away, and worship other gods and serve them, I announce to you today that you shall surely perish; you shall not prolong your days in the land . . . " Let us look at the process. First, there is a turning away from God and God's commandments. How does that happen, you say? It begins with a lie; not a public lie, but a private lie. It might be something like this: "I do not need to be honest in my dealings with my teachers. I can save time by browsing the Internet and copying the writings of others for my papers. My professor will never know." However, once you begin to cheat you get caught up in the cheating and continue to do so. After a while, it seems you have gotten away with it, but in your heart, deceit has been given a corner to live. You then cheat in other areas of your life. Now it is a public lie! After a while, you are nothing but a cheat. Every relationship that you establish is laden with this cheating spirit. Very soon, you begin to think, "Wow, this is cool, why didn't I think of this before?" My brother, you are being drawn away from God, and toward death. Not just death in the traditional sense. Most of us think about death as the separation of this life from the body. Well, that is a death, but it is not the only death. Death also occurs when you are separated from your true self. When you choose to be something other than your Creator wanted for you, you are dead to the possibilities available in God.

Once your heart turns away from God and you are drawn away by the lie, it is only a small step to worshiping other gods. "Come on, preacher, no one is foolish enough to worship other gods!" What do you call the lust for money, power, women, sex, and material things? First you worship them and then you serve them! You may not call it worship, though. It starts as a desire to have things. There is nothing wrong in wanting things. Yet, when your desire is to have things just to prove your worth, or women to prove your manhood, or power so you can get back at people or inflict your will on others, you are turning away from the natural design and its Designer! When you will do anything to accrue or get those things, then in my book you are worshiping and serving other gods. Think about it. It is called idolatry. That is what it's called when we worship things and not the Creator God, who makes all things possible in this universe.

Another example, if you don't mind: a brother (or a sister) starts out snorting cocaine occasionally. Then, after a time, she doesn't need an occasion to get high—she just does it. You begin to get a little lax about going to class, about your hygiene or anything that is not directly related to getting high. You are only a small step from addiction, or the worship of a drug. When you worship drugs, you will do whatever is necessary, including theft, to acquire them. Is that not serving them? If you will lie, steal, or deceive others to get something, you are serving that thing as a god. How many of you know a drug addict? Will they steal from you? Will they steal from their momma to get a fix? Case closed!

How many of you know a sex addict? That is someone who will do whatever is necessary to get with somebody. If they are sitting next to you do not look at them, but you can give them a nudge. Nevertheless, a sex addict does not care who the other person is or whether they are in a relationship with someone; all they care about is taking care of their addiction. That, my sister, is serving another god. That person is serving the god of lust. Can I get a witness up in here?

That is the other side of the story. Perhaps I went to the extreme in creating images you could easily recognize. So what about those persons who don't get caught up in the extremes of life? You know, the everyday folks who may lie a little bit, you know, about little stuff. Persons who cheat a little bit, you know, who might look over at a friend's paper during an exam. Or persons who may "forget" to tell the new boy in physics they are in a relationship, as he asks for their number with that drop-dead gorgeous smile. Or they may steal every once in a while, but not habitually. You know, like when they are out having fun they'll maybe take a candy bar or something. What about them, you know, people like you and I? What God has for those persons is still secure, right? Well, yes and no!

The good news is that God is available to forgive and cleanse us of all unrighteousness. The good news is that whatever you have done in life, God blesses you in spite of it. However, I need you to remember that the blessings are a part of a formula that requires obedience as a pre-condition. Therefore, whenever we determine in our hearts that we will obey, the blessings begin to flow from that point. Are you feeling me?

God is not a puppet master, dangling our lives on a string for us to jump. Nor do we live in a vacuum, immune from the decisions of others in our lives. You see, life is a complicated endeavor, not a simple thing. Let me give you some possible scenarios to highlight what I am trying to explain. Let's say, for example, that a boy grows up in a godly household, yet picks up bad habits from his associates in the community. Those habits begin to define who he is. God will not override those habits to demonstrate His power, as that would be a violation of free will. Depending on how long those habits matriculate in that life, some possibilities are lost forever! Whenever that young man decides to choose another path and begin to follow God with all his heart, then his real life begins. Still, some of those previous choices follow him. God will forgive the sin of those previous actions, but the consequences of our acts follow us. If he was a 'dog' and has fathered children by many women, that takes away from his witness, eats up potential resources for other things, and creates an environment for those children to live in poverty or wards of the State. Yet, he is forgiven! In that scenario, he probably thought school was a joke, so he did not apply himself to learning. So now he is saved, but he is also poorly prepared to be an asset to the society. God wants to bless him, but he has limited the areas of the blessing. If he has been incarcerated, then he has further limited God. What we fail to realize is that the consequences of our actions limit what God can do on our behalf. To expect God to blot out our past is not realistic! Yet we can expect that God, through Christ, will work on our behalf in spite of our past.

Yes, the real Good News is that in spite of our past, God will make a way out of no way, if we are faithful. The way may not be like that made for another, but God will make a way. We have choices all along life's highway. Therefore, when God sees that we are serious, He will step in. God will create favor for those who love Him and are willing to be obedient. That is why the scripture says: "Work out your own salvation with trembling and fear." The Spirit wants to work on our behalf, but we must also do our part. That part is the active Word in our lives, faith in a Risen Savior who does all things well and a life set apart for God and dead to self. To the degree that these things are active and visible in your life, then the power of God is available to work on your behalf. That is the Good News of Jesus Christ: That while we were yet sinners, Christ died for us. Though our sins be as scarlet, He can clean the slate of the penalty. We don't have to settle for the consequences of sin. Still, in order to overcome the consequences in our life we must work while it is day, for night cometh when no man can work. Remember that when Satan came to God with the tests for Job, God testified to the character of Job. Faith gives you character. Character says, "This is who I am. I am standing on the promises of almighty God. I am not standing on my looks, intelligence, heritage, or wealth. I am standing on the promises of God. Thus, I am more than a conqueror. I will, through Jesus the Christ, overcome my past. I will, through the working of the Holy Spirit, claim a godly character. I will, through my faith in God, become a blessing to those around me. I will trust in the Lord. I will trust in the Lord. I said, I will trust in the Lord." Is there someone else in the house that will also begin to trust in the Lord? Are there some persons here today who will step out on faith and try God? I mean really try God? From wherever you are, step out and give me your hand and give God your heart. Don't wait until a better time. Today is the acceptable time and now is the acceptable hour. Is there one? If you are afraid to walk by yourself, I will come and meet you. However, don't allow the devil to continue to take the glory out of your life; that is designed only for God. Come, oh come ye blessed of my Father. Come and receive the blessing that has been waiting for you since the day you were born. Come! Amen.

In retrospect, I may have looked at another way of addressing an unspoken concern of many in the fellowship. However, the events of the coming week stretched our resolve. As the date suggests, all hell was about to break loose. Where was God in all of this? How does love and grace factor into our understanding of our sense of reality? Tuesday, September 11th caught us unaware. More persons came seeking answers than we had counselors to sit with them. Our Listening Post was set up in the Student Center and was in full swing. I received a call at home to come and energize the Emergency Response Team.

When I arrived on Campus, Gretta Barnes and Lyn Gulledge were busy trying to keep up with the traffic of people seeking comfort. I called the Psychology Department to get assistance but it was slow in responding. Meanwhile, I called several local Pastors requesting them to join us in grief counseling. That day, we saw over four hundred persons, including faculty and staff. In addition to prayer vigils, we opened phone banks for students to reach out, mediated discussions and generally wept with every crying person on Campus. Wednesday provided an opportunity to worship and we were overwhelmed with the attendance. Love and grace was my theme for the week.

That Tuesday, Wednesday, and again on Thursday we held service. People were outwardly shaken and some voiced the fear that we were about to be invaded. It did not help that the media repeatedly showed the images of the crashes. I wish that I had written the messages because they were very well received. Sunday would be the culmination of the week and I was drained. What would I say that would offer grace in the midst of trouble?

Sermon: Sunday, September 16, 2001
Psalm 121

Our sense of well being, the comfort of our daily existence, has been dealt a devastating blow. First, we encountered the attacks of September 11th, a day permanently etched in our minds. Our initial reaction was one of disbelief that something of this magnitude could happen here. Then we became conscious of a personal terror because loved ones were either working nearby or at the sites of devastation. To compound the matter, we had to endure the continuous news-breaking footage shown until our senses were almost numb. Yet, after sifting through the various layers of conflicting emotions, shedding many tears, and leaning on one another, we began to move to another place.

For me, that place is in the Word of God. This is where I find words of assurance in a troubling time. Here I find the psalmist speaking, as it were, directly to me. His words of settling the source of my help are transforming and potent for the issue facing me. For after the Word returns me to the source, my God, I can venture into the world to hear the objections being raised, and the issues being discussed.

As I listen to the voices in the marketplace of ideas, I hear voices of prayerful concern and also the voices of vengeance. For many, the practice of prayer brought them comfort; for others, the idea of revenge energized their being.

Their prayers and mine were intended to be of an intercessory nature, for the families of this tragedy. We felt their pain because it was our pain. We wanted the families to know they were not alone in their mourning. We wanted the world to know that we stood together as one. In addition, the prayers were also for us. We were shaken, and rightly so. Our silent prayer was simple: "Lord, keep us safe."

For those who moved toward the specter of revenge, the dominant theme was outrage. Their sense of invincibility had been shattered and they wanted to have an identifiable enemy against which to strike. The young men on this Campus were among the first to express this emotion to me. Yet for many, an incongruity of emotions was evidently at work. For a while they wanted the military to strike back decisively. They also had personal fears to overcome. Their dilemma as members of the National Guard was the fear of being called to active duty. Any activation of troops would probably involve them and some were not adequately prepared for this eventuality. Therefore, by day, the talk revolved around a strike against the enemy; at night, they spoke chillingly with loved ones and their Campus Minister about staying in school and away from the battlefront. The delay of troop deployment helped to ease building tension and provided time for the others to get ready. Therefore, my task is to say a word that speaks to the core. The psalmist reminds us: "My help comes from the Lord."

Consequently, we come today looking for assurance. In our return to God's word, I invite your attention to these words: "I lift up my eyes to the hills. From whence does my help come? My help comes from the Lord, who made heaven and earth." As we approach this word today let us be honest before God and ask that all our issues be resolved. We come with battered psyches, bruised egos and mounting fears. We come with questions of why, how and what next. Even in the midst of trouble, I must assert: My help comes from God! Yes, I confess that I am afraid. Still, my help comes from God. You may ask, "Why are you so adamant about this, Rev?" Let me give you three reasons why God is my help in the time of trouble.

My immediate reply is that God is vigilant. The psalmist declares: "Behold, he who keeps Israel will neither slumber nor sleep." In other words, God is constantly on guard. That's 24/7! 365! No off days. No down time.

Secondly, the Psalmist adds: "The Lord is your keeper; the Lord is your shade on your right hand." At this point I want you to recognize that God has keeping power. Protection avails itself so that-"Neither the sun by day, nor the moon by night" allows the enemy to get to you. In the shadow of his right hand, I am secure. As I think about the tragedies that have occurred in our nation, I recognize that some persons may question these statements of mine. They will say, "If that is so, then what happened?" My answer is that we have not seen the final scene yet. Do not write off this scene just yet! Our God is still on the throne and the final script has not yet been played out. You see, my help is not limited to this veil of tears. There is another day coming when God shall right the wrongs. There is another day coming when Jesus shall crack open the sky and the dead in Christ shall rise first. My hope is not just in this realm, but also in another realm "where the wicked shall cease from troubling and the weary shall be at rest."

In addition, I know God is present because of the guidance he offers. The psalmist says, "The Lord will keep you from all evil; he will keep your life." In other words, God guides me away from evil. In so doing, there is protection from the enemy and also from myself. By keeping my going out and my coming in, God keeps me away from the lures that so easily beset me! The songwriter puts it this way: "From dangers seen and unseen, God keeps us." We can see the same thought echoed in the Gospel of Matthew, where the disciples ask Jesus to teach them how to pray. His response: "Lead us not into temptation; but deliver us from evil." Why? Because he knew that there were situations where, if encountered, we could not handle them victoriously. Therefore, our prayer should be, "Lord, help me to avoid that snare, that trap." In other words, if we know that pleasing our peers IS high on our agenda for life, then sometimes we may have to avoid their activities. If every time we see that piece of "eye candy" we get weak in the knees and a flame ignites our hearts, we are in trouble. We need to avoid being alone with them either until we learn to control our emotions, or until we get married! It is as simple as that!

Therefore, your prayer should be, "Lord, you know! Help me to avoid being alone with them. I cannot handle it. Lead me away from that evil. Protect me from myself!" Is there a witness in here? Is there anyone seeing themselves in a new light? Are you willing to admit what you see in this area of your life? Won't God help you if you ask?

Finally, as I bring this message to an end, I am drawn to this statement: "from this time forth and forevermore." The writer is attuned to us and wants to leave an impression with us. Yes, these are difficult days we are facing. Yes, it is uncharted territory for most of us. Still, the psalmist profoundly reminds us, "God will be there for you!" This is neither the time nor the place to give up or give in to terror. When your fears make you feel like you are helpless, remember, God is still help for the helpless, still hope for the hopeless! If no one stands with you and you are left to fend for yourself, God is still a friend to the friendless and will not forsake you. Not only is God with you today but he is with you forevermore. Friends, this is not the time to question your faith or the time to throw in the towel. Even when buildings are crumbling from terrorist activities, I will trust Him. Even when planes are falling from the sky with deadly impact, I will trust Him. This is the time to hold on, the time to be strong. Our God is able to hold us in the hollow of His unchanging Hands. Even when this body dies and is put into the ground, I will trust him! For my faith tells me flesh and blood cannot inherit eternal life. No, this mortal must put on immortality. I will trust God to watch over me, even as I await the coming of my Lord. Amen.

As I look back, I see that this was not only an opportunity to minister a word of comfort but also a chance to reinforce some core beliefs. The crowd swelled to one hundred and eighty five for this gathering, and many were challenged by this message. I am convinced that too much was going on to receive it all; yet I believe that subconsciously it was received. The ensuing week saw a partial return to normalcy. However, the additional threat of anthrax added anxiety to the already heightened sense of unrest on Campus. I became fully aware that many were not equipped to handle the levels of stress they faced. In addition, I sensed that many urgently wanted to gain some level of faith to undergird their fears. Although I don't relish 'battle field' conversions, I wanted to present a message that was basic in content, yet latent with grace and hope. Therefore, I sought the Lord for a word to speak. My thoughts would not leave DD and perhaps, the following sermon had him in mind.

Sermon: "The Peril of Oneness"
II Kings 5:1-15

September 23, 2001

The story of Naaman is here for a number of reasons. However, today we want to look at how God uses others in our lives. The text says that Naaman had it going on. He was the commander of the army, a great man, had the respect of his king, had the favor of the Lord, but was a leper. So he was not perfect. The story reminds us that we all have something wrong with us. It may be slight, nearly unseen, but there is always something not quite right. My flaw may not be your flaw, but we are all flawed. Regardless of how beautiful you may be, you are not flawless. No matter how suave and debonair you think you are, there is something amiss. You may have it going on off the hook, but there is a virus in your software—and that makes you imperfect.

Recognizing this, we must endeavor to not let our flaw hold us back or to prevent the major blessing God has for us. Naaman had a flaw. His flaw was leprosy. Now this did not prevent him from becoming a general in the army, a great man or being blessed of God. It did, however, define him. (Is there an event in your life that has defined you?)

Now, during a raid upon Israel he had good fortune. In this raid he captured a Hebrew maiden. This was good fortune because she was aware of something that was important to him and he didn't even know it. You see, although he had been blessed of God, he did not know God and the awesome power that was available through God. Turn to your neighbor and say, "Neighbor, even though you may not know God for yourself, he can still bless you." Naaman did not know God, but God blessed him anyhow! God allowed him to have the victory over Israel, even though Israel was His chosen people. You see, when sin is in the mix, God will sometimes chastise you. So God used Naaman and the Syrian army to chastise Israel for failing to be obedient to the Word and way of God.

As Providence would have it, this little Israelite girl, though a servant, is treated well by the household. So well that in her normal conversation, she tells Mrs. Naaman about a prophet of her God who lives in Israel. When you are in a position of power, it helps to treat other folk well. Turn to your neighbor and say, "Neighbor, even though you are 'the man,' treat your neighbor right." So Naaman hears about this prophet and immediately goes to his king with the news. His king gets excited and sends Naaman to the king of Israel with a request for healing. The king did not send him empty-handed, either. He did not come begging, but had a reward for the expected service. Just because you are excited about the possibilities available in God, don't think everyone else shares your optimism. Somebody will rain on your parade with his or her personal negative vibes. Naaman goes to the Israelite king with gifts and great expectations only to find the king of Israel suspicious and afraid. He thinks this is a ploy to find an excuse for another war against him, so the King tears his clothes, and begins to wail loudly in the court. But God has a different idea. The word gets to Elisha what has transpired and Elisha tells the king, "Send him to me and I'll show him God has a prophet in Israel." The king is relieved and sends brother Naaman to the prophet.

However, a funny thing happened. When Naaman arrived at Elisha's door with his caravan of horses and chariots, the prophet does not answer his call. Instead, he sends a servant out with directions for his cure. This infuriates Naaman. His pride gets the best of him and he loses it. I understand how the brother felt. After all, he was a conquering general. It must have humiliated him to travel from his home in Syria to Israel, the place of a defeated people, then go before the king of Israel and be sent somewhere else, where the host of the house did not even come out to greet him. I understand how he felt! The text reminds us not to get so excited about our circumstances that we miss out on our blessing. Naaman's anger is about to cause him to overlook his blessing, and his national pride is fueling the fire. He says, " I thought he would at least come out to me . . . wave his hands over my disease . . . and besides, the rivers of Syria are better." He is hurt. He wants to have a pity party.

Then one of his traveling companions helps him out. "Mr. Naaman, sir, if he had told you to do something spectacular, wouldn't you have done it? So why not just wash in the Jordan and be healed?" Sometimes, we need another person to help us to see the light. There are times when our circumstances or our personal conflicts blind us to the blessing right in front of us. I believe God uses ordinary people to help us along this journey—if we would only pay attention. Naaman listened and was healed. But the story does not end there. After he was healed, he returned to the prophet of God to say thank you and to give God some praise. Turn to your neighbor and say, "Neighbor, when the Lord blesses you, you ought to praise Him and give thanks."

There is a story of two high school boys, George and Stephen. George was frail but Stephen was an athlete. One day, Stephen saw George taking books home on a Friday afternoon and thought, "What a nerd." Yet as he looked at the heavy load of items, he decided to offer a hand. They walked together and Stephen talked about his goal of being a professional football player. George didn't say much but was glad for the company. This was the first person at this school to reach out to him, and he was grateful for the attention. As they approached his home, George stopped and thanked Stephen for his help again. Then he gathered the items from him and struggled the rest of the way alone. Stephen thought this was strange but did not object since he had already passed his home. He turned with a bright smile and told him that he would see him on Monday. After walking a few feet, he stopped and asked if he would like to hang with him tomorrow. There was a party to attend. George almost stumbled at the good news and said, "Sure." Well, they hung out that Saturday night and many more nights after that during their high school years.

Finally, graduation approached and George and Stephen were being honored. Both were going to college: Stephen as an All American football player and George on an academic scholarship. In addition, George was valedictorian and was scheduled to give a brief address. In his opening words, he thanked his parents for their love and support as expected. Then he did an unexpected thing. He thanked Stephen for saving his life. You see, that Friday they met, he was clearing out his locker because he was going to kill himself. Stephen had showed him kindness and friendship in the midst of his pity party. That was the difference in his living and not taking his life as he had planned. You see, he thought he was weird and didn't deserve to live. However, a kind word and a friendly deed changed his mind. You never know who you might touch with an act of kindness.

Naaman and George had something in common, though they never knew each other. An unexpected person reached out on their behalf and God was then able to bless them in spite of their flaw. The blessing was waiting for an initiator to get the ball rolling. In one life it was a servant girl. In the other's life it was a football player. Each of us, every day, has the opportunity to be used by God to bless a life. What reason will we give today for not doing so? Why not be used by God and see His glory revealed in a life? Amen.

I revived this sermon, at least partially, because I could not get DD out of my mind. Another factor in my consideration was how to address the lingering war motif that some members of the fellowship exhibited. Subconsciously, I was dealing with my own anxieties about the attacks on Afghanistan and the rhetoric being espoused about a just and holy war. It made me sick because I sensed that the American public was being manipulated and the 'enemy' was being demonized/dehumanized.

When the person being attacked is less than human, it assuages the conscience of the attacker and may even justify the attack at some level. Finally, I had thoughts about the innocent being victimized with no voice raised for them. Especially of concern to me were the workers at National Airport who had been furloughed without any benefits, yet the airlines had received billions of dollars worth of aid. Not lost in my thoughts were the women and children of Afghanistan, though the innocent were being murdered by errant bullets and bomb and at least were displaced by the activities of war.

Verbatim: JF

JF is a 19 year-old sophomore from Hampton. I received a call from a professor familiar with our ministry with a request for personal counseling. All she would say was that this young lady was depressed and not working up to her potential. I did not recognize the name and was surprised when I saw her that she was a 'lost sheep' from the previous fall. She had been a regular in attendance at our Sunday services but had not returned this year. I was not certain if she was still in school or had been swallowed up by the young men on Campus. The first year can be a difficult period of adjustment for the young adults, especially the women. They have a freedom most have never experienced, the young men are very attentive, and the attention can be addictive. Many drop out at the end of the first semester/year due to pregnancies. When JE arrived at my office, there were three of 'my children' present so we went across the hall to the Chapel.

> JF: Hello, Rev. JD. Do you remember me?
> Rev: Yes, but it's been awhile since I have seen you. What's been going on?
> JF: Well, I have been going home a lot. My boyfriend wants me to be with him so I have been going home.
> Rev: I see. Are you involved with a church at home?
> JF: Well, kind of...I go sometimes, but lately I been sleepy a lot, so I just rest.
> Rev: So, what brings you this way today?
> JF: My math professor suggested I come and talk with you. I want to drop that class.

Rev: Well, you can do that if necessary. Tell me, why do you want to drop?

JF: I have never been good in math and I don't feel like doing the work. Besides, it is not like I am going to need this stuff in life, you know?

Rev: What, you mean you won't need quantum physics?

JF: Funny. It's not physics, it's math!

Rev: I know. Just wanted to lighten the mood some. You are so serious.

JF: I have got a lot going on and I don't need this math thing.

Rev: What do you want to share today? Obviously, this is not just about math. If that was the case, you could just fill out the paperwork and it would be a done deal. What's really happening with you?

JF: I am so confused right now. I am pregnant! My folks are so disappointed with me and I am not ready for this. I told you I have been going home a lot and that's the problem. My boyfriend loves me but is in no position to take care of a baby. He stays with his mother and she is tripping. She is trying to take charge of my life already ... suggesting names for the baby, offering us a place in her home, and stuff like that. My education is important!

Rev: I see. What do you want to do?

JF: I want to stay with my parents, have the baby, and finish school. My folks are both retired from the military and are willing to help me. I can get a job and go to school in the evenings. My mom is willing to baby-sit while I am at school. I would transfer to Old Dominion because it's closer to home and most of my classes would be in the evening. I am too young to get married and all that.

Rev: How does the young man feel about all this?

JF: He will do whatever I want to do. He's an only child and his mother rules him. She told him to ask me to marry him, so he did. But he's out of work right now and I can't see that. Besides, I don't want to get married. I thought about having an abortion but decided that was not right. I made a mistake, so I have to pay the penalty!

Rev: Is that you talking or your folks?

JF: A little of both! They don't believe in abortion and neither do I. I was so stupid to get myself in this mess!
What should I do?

Rev: I can't tell you what to do. That's up to you. However, if
you have not been to see a doctor, I would advise that be
at the top of your list. It's good idea to make certain that
you get good prenatal care. You know, get your vitamin
supplements and stuff like that.

JF: You sound like my mother. Yes, I have had a visit already and the baby is developing well. I did not use
my parent's health plan for that visit because I did not
want them to find out like that. My boyfriend, well,
probably his mother, paid for the check-up. Although I
am just at the end of my first trimester, everything
looks good.

Rev: You know I am going to ask, right? What were you
thinking about since you know you don't want to be a
mother? All sorts of protection are available, even here
at college, for free.

JF: I know. I am so stupid!

Rev: Let's call it a bad decision instead.

JF: No, I was stupid.

Rev: Ok, You were stupid. But let's not take all the blame for
this bad decision. You were not alone. This is shared responsibility, just like the parenting of the child should
become. Are you all right with that last part?

JF: Yes, as long as his mother does not try to take over.

Rev: I am sure you will not allow that to happen.

JF: Rev JD, I have got to run. Thanks for taking the time to talk
with me. I know I have not been available for Bible study or
Sunday Chapel, but I am going to try to attend soon.

I have not seen her since, nor did I expect to see her. Her
story is a microcosm of what is happening at many universities.
They come with naive notions of their vulnerability to the reali-
ties of life and then wonder what happened. If I have heard the
story once, I have heard it a hundred times. It is always an unexpected pregnancy; yet, there is no attempt to use
contraceptives. As I wrestle with this matter, I see grace in action. The fact that there are not more pregnancies, for there are

certainly a multitude of couples engaging in unprotected sex, shouts grace. Even with the rise of STDs, denial shouts: "It won't happen to me, I am invincible. Those things happen to other people." Well, to other people, they are the other people. As I reflect upon my own life, I can see the same naïveté in my own self. So I understand, and yet I don't. This generation has far more information than we did. Nevertheless, they continue to repeat the mistakes of their parents, just as I did. Maybe it speaks to our humanity: we see what we want to see when we want to see it.

However, they also had a vision of the future. Most managed to escape the limitations imposed by segregated schools with poor facilities and makeshift resources, and to succeed, at least to this point, in pursuing their education. "Today, years later, all big-city school systems are largely black and failing; whites and middle class blacks have fled to the suburbs or private schools. Indeed, effective school integration today is a myth. Instead of attending warm and dynamic schools where they are sponsored and affirmed, black students today are educationally crippled, too often abandoned in urban, drug-infested, violent, crime-ridden holding pens and dealt with like cattle."[4]

We cannot undo the past. We cannot wipe away the stains of former hurts or failures. What we can do is instill hope. What we can do is share with them the beauty as revealed unto us by Christ and nurture their sense of expectancy. When we see the flame spark we can fan that ember, hoping for an eruption to occur. Even if we don't see it, we have hope that it will occur. Without the grace of God, where would we be? We attempted to be the nurturing environment that many of these students needed. I believe we succeeded, at least for some. We now look closer at the development of nurture.

---

[4] Proctor, Samuel DeWitt. *The Substance of Things Hoped For: A Memoir of African-American Faith* (New York: G.P. Putnam's Sons, 1996), 68.

CHAPTER 3

Nurture: A function of hospitality

If hospitality is the intentional welcoming of persons into your space, then nurture is the integral component in that process. Nurture is a word often used to mean to take care of another. I also extend it to mean to draw a person close enough that they are aware you are caring for them. If you are unaware of the concept, it may seem peculiar that a stranger would intentionally go out of his or her way to welcome you. Yet that is exactly what occurred. In so doing, I believe we were carrying on a multi-dimensional aspect of the traditional African American church. Dr. Sam Roberts puts it this way: "...the Christian churches have always been at their best when they gathered believers into a nurturing environment that facilitated praise of God, faithful living in the world, and reassuring care of each believer."[5] Upon reflection, it is very evident that as an extension of that church our Campus Ministry has experienced nurture. Not only in assisting our students in transition, but also this minister. Nurture was necessary to counter the many negative experiences of life and in the formulation of a positive response to what was happening in, through and with those involved. Nurture informed my preaching, teaching, and social interactions.

However, nurture is not a one-way street, nor is she one-dimensional. Board members, a Clinical Pastoral Class, and

---

[5] Roberts, Samuel K. *African American Christian Ethics.* (Cleveland: The Pilgrim Press, 2001), 182. This book informs my understanding of alienation, reconciliation, and redemption as played out in the African American community.

when allowed, students also provided nurturing for themselves and for me. After a brief description of the ways I was involved I will move to the Board members, the CPE class, and then the students.

A discipline I have followed faithfully is the taking of photographs of the young adults whenever they gathered. Later in the same week, I would proudly display the pictures on our bulletin board. It provided to passers-by and returning participants a view of those who had been present. It indicated that we cared enough about them to note their coming and sharing in the event. Students would gather around the photos on display and point with pride to themselves or would ask me to please take down a particular photograph. This was nurture. They felt comfortable in approaching me about any subject because they felt they knew me. I cannot emphasize that enough. Maybe I did not remember their names all the time but I knew their faces and remembered their stories. It also helped me to note the faces of those coming regularly and to intentionally get to know them much better. As I walked around the Campus, I could engage them specifically about a point made in the service or question them about their opinion on an issue. My walks around Campus were purposeful and directed towards reacquainting myself with students who had been at a gathering, gleaning information as to what was happening in their lives and introducing myself to new students. However, being the caretaker for many requires energy and when I was drained, I needed that special care. There were those who nurtured me so I could be available to others. The Board of Directors was available for me in many ways, and I need to highlight the varied ways they nurtured me. Each came with unique gifts and graces that were vitally needed when they surfaced. The Providential care of God was manifested through their care for the ministry and for me. In this space, however, I will only share glimpses of the Board Chairs.

Board of Directors

Mr. Herbert Coulton of First Baptist Church, Petersburg, served as my initial Board Chair and began a pattern of nurture that for me has been invaluable. I inherited him from Mrs. Adams, and his extensive community experience has been instrumental in getting the ministry recognized beyond the island of VSU. As a former Field Secretary for the Southern Christian Leadership Conference (SCLC) and friend of Dr. Martin Luther King, Jr., his community contacts are awesome. He was able to take this preacher places where an outsider could not go and make him feel at home there. In addition, Herb is a layperson and genuinely nurtures preachers in general and this minister in particular. He was instrumental in getting the ministry on the budget of his local church and set a standard for the other board members. In that sense, he also nurtured the ministry in its infancy, providing financial stability. He has since been relegated to Emeritus status, but the gift of his person is still available to me whenever I need a sounding board. And, First Baptist Church gives more to this ministry than any local church.

The Reverend Dr. Michael A. Battle, Jr. came to us from Hampton University after serving the ministry there for more than 25 years. His arrival coincided with new energy fueled by Herb and others. As Associate V.P. for Student Affairs he provided oversight for the ministry. In addition, he served as Board Chair briefly and as my mentor. Although the setting was different, his experience in ministry and his familiarity with the local ministers provided a different access for the ministry and additional credibility. During his brief tenure, we were able to co-host some significant events that brought well-respected ministers to the Campus, garner newspaper coverage and boost our visibility with the larger student body. In all of this I received the credit; but he did the work and wanted to be left in the background. I owe him a great debt of gratitude for the unselfish service he rendered for this ministry. Finally, an offer came his way that he could not refuse. But prior to his departure, he choreographed a scene where I became the interim pastor for an historical church in Petersburg. Although this required more work on my part, it also gave me a larger stage to make my case for Campus Ministry to the community at large. I could not have pulled that off without his assistance. Dr. Battle now serves as President of the Interdenominational Theological Center in Atlanta, GA.

Dr. Gilbert Gipson is a faculty member of VSU, and succeeded Dr. Battle as Board Chair. One Sunday he simply showed up before the worship began and asked if I would like instrumental music for the service. It was an unanswered prayer of mine, and in he walked with instruments in tow. This immediately added a depth to our corporate worship that was marvelous. If you have ever struggled to lead worship without an organist or keyboard, then you understand. Initially, he brought his own keyboard. Then when we were able to purchase an instrument, I utilized his expertise in securing the best product within our budget. For the next two and a half years, he played keyboard for us. To have a faculty member do this was remarkable! For one, he never shared his gift with me prior to that Sunday, though he was faithful during that stint of time. It was the missing ingredient to our worship experience. He has since yielded to students playing at the worship service but does occasionally sit in to encourage us and ensure continuity. On occasion I still call on him when the students inform me of their unavailability to play.

Dr. Jimmie L. Battle, our current Chair, is a retired faculty member and a member of Alpha Kappa Sorority, Inc. She is also a layperson, a member of the Board of Deacons at Gillfield Baptist Church and an ardent supporter of this ministry. When we were soliciting fraternal support, both sororities and fraternities, for the furnishing of the Chapel, her advice was invaluable. Yet, following those males, her nurture is of a different nature. She will bake cookies for me and invite me to relax and have quiet conversation. Don't think, however, that she is soft—far from it. Those conversations are sessions where I derive invaluable guidance, counsel and suggestions about possible initiatives.

Board Members

Dr. Jimmie L. Battle The Honorable Y. Robinson
Ms. Carmencita Stewart
Mr. Michael Coleman
Mrs. Victoria Adams,
EmeritusHerbert Coulton, Emeritus
Ms. M. Rene Arnold

Ms. Gretta Barnes
Ms. Dana Cephas
Mr. David E. Clarke, III
Dr. Gilbert Gipson
Pastor Alice B. Gray
Rev. Rebecca Griffin
Ms. Sylmereial Higgins
Rev. Martha P. Jenkins
Col. Melvin Jones
Mr. Reginald Knotts
Dr. Mel Krohn
Mr. Abraham Maven
Mrs. Gloria Nolan
Dr. George Partin
Mrs. Ann C. Taylor
Rev. Wm. Anthony Layman

I do not wish to imply that only the chairpersons are engaged in this ministry. The members of the board are not only indispensable but also provide nurture, financial support and guidance. They are the unsung heroes working behind the scenes, ensuring tasks are accomplished, budgets are met, bills are paid, and events adequately planned. I salute all of them because without their tireless efforts and prayers we would not be doing this work so admirably.

As I continue to reflect upon the project and the period shared, I must turn to an unexpected source of nurture for me. (Reflection is a useful tool, because you can sift through materials and extrapolate the essence from the events without telling the entire story.) The providence of God was guiding me in a needed direction with forces I could not control. As I delved into deep waters with students, that step was also needed in my personal journey. In walked Clinical Pastoral Education to meet that need.

Clinical Pastoral Education (CPE)

On my journey in becoming the person I am, I was required by my denomination (United Methodist) to participate in a course of Clinical Pastoral Education (CPE). It is a process of getting to know oneself better, bringing some personal issues to resolution, and serving in a setting that is clinical. By that I mean we engage in ministry in a supervised setting designed to stretch, educate, and refine our pastoral skills. I did not expect that this environment would also be nurturing to myself and the others engaged in the course. In fact, it may prove to be the most beneficial component in my personal development.

During five months of daily activity, we interacted with each other in love, but with an eye to the correction of any pattern of behaviors indicating transference of any sort, that we were unusually defensive of, and seemed to have undue emotional attachment. The group, under the direction of Dr. Harry Simmons, was instructed to challenge these actions during our presentation of information relating to the class, as a result of our interactions with patients. The belief in force was that if we displayed these attributes in that setting, then they were probably in our interactions in our ministerial settings.

Transference occurs when the individual transfers emotional baggage or experience into a situation that does not merit it. For example, my pain of separation from my father was a wound that had not sufficiently healed to allow me to move forward in a healthy manner. Hence, whenever I was engaged in pastoral care of young men, my emotional baggage clouded our interactions and I projected unnecessary issues into the relationship. If it had not been brought to my attention by this class, I would have continued in that fashion. It was unhealthy and did nothing to help the young men to resolve their conflicts. Once I was made aware, however, I was able to stop and see their situation for what it was, without my transferred baggage.

The particular case that made me aware of this issue in my life involved reporting a visit I made to the Spinal Cord Unit. A young veteran had been injured in an accident. He was being treated at Hunter McGuire Medical Center and I went to see him. While there, we bonded, and he shared parts of his story with me. He was 19 and had recently lost his father to alcohol-related complications. He was very forthcoming, relating in detail the activities he had shared with his father, including a dinner prior to his last illness and subsequent death. In talking about this visit I became very emotional and froze when questioned about it. I could not explain what was happening and was reluctant to investigate my emotions. Yet, after a friend in the class was willing to share his pain of separation concerning his father, I was freed to do likewise.

My father died from alcoholism when I was 19 years old. We had not seen each other for more than ten years and I had only vague memories of him. Yet I loved him, and recalled attending the funeral on my way to Viet Nam. During all those years, I had not brought closure to his death and had additional issues with him, primarily regarding his absence from my life. In addition, I was blaming him for not being a person which he was incapable of being. After processing this I was able to mourn his passing and offer forgiveness. I needed to move forward; after all, the man had been dead for 30 years. Yet, when visiting with the young vet, all of this surfaced. The group nurtured me through this buried emotional baggage, which had been weighing me down and was hindering healing on a personal level. They allowed me to grieve his loss and be comforted. I needed that! Afterward, I was able to return to the young vet and offer appropriate comfort without my baggage interfering with the process.

On a variety of occasions all of us were subjected to this type of scrutiny, and much healing occurred during those months. In all fairness, I should say that healing began in those areas of our lives. At another, deeper level, friendships were formed and nurtured as we cared for each other and found a safe place to share our pain, disappointments and our hope for the future. Especially rewarding were our Monday devotions after a weekend of duty covering the Medical Center. We were required to provide coverage on a rotating basis and the weekends were always eventful.

Since that time, I attend personal growth retreats to continue to understand who I am and the pain that has helped me toward consciousness. In addition, the process continues to unfold as books are introduced and read, teaching opportunities present themselves, and the Holy Spirit uses all of me, at least the portions of which I am aware and willing to let go for the greater good. The final component that I will examine is the manner in which students provided nurture for me.

The Students of Campus Ministry

From the initial gathering in 1998, five of those gathered have stepped forth and assumed leadership positions. In addition, for the next three years they attended our leadership retreats, Wednesday Fellowship and Sunday Worship and were a constant presence in the Center. They became recruiters of students, visionaries of what the ministry could/should become, ushers and worship leaders, liaisons with their peers, and nurturers of this minister.

At the leadership retreats, they selected the subject areas, assisted the presenters, kept me awake, and made certain all the students were actively engaged. In other words, they made my task easy. Did I mention that they also recruited students to attend? I learned from them that students came to hang out with each other, not to hear a particular presenter.

I will admit that at our initial retreat, November 1998, I did all the planning and made the necessary arrangements (including transportation and presenters); but after following me, I challenged them to lead. I shared with them the process, gave suggestive guidelines, and recommended presenters and topics; but they made the selections. Once they had experienced a successful retreat, their esteem received a boost and their confidence level was unmatched. I literally watched them grow before my eyes. It was after the 1999 retreat that they began to talk about going to Africa! Once their confidence level was raised, their sense of self also increased. Now they truly believed that they could do anything.

Regarding the Wednesday Night Fellowship, we formatted the service to include a period of testimony similar to the

Sunday service. Their idea was that students want to praise even if they don't know much about the Bible. I acquiesced and we found a mutually accepted medium. Persons would share their testimonies, sing songs of praise, and invite others to do the same. (After this group graduated in 2002, I was forced to make several adjustments because the testimonies had become mini-sermons and the invitation to join in bordered on a command!)

Yet while it lasted, it was an enjoyable fellowship. Their testimonies were riveting because although so much had happened in their young lives, they still had hope. To see this large group standing, clapping and praising God nurtured my spirit. They created an environment that facilitated preaching. I saw the Spirit of God working in their lives, and we averaged 125 persons at the Sunday service and 35 at the mid-week setting.

When the worship was over, they helped to serve the snacks, engaged each other in conversation and affirmed the preacher, whether it was a guest minister or myself. Before leaving the building, they made certain the area was neat and presentable.

The Ministry Center became their home away from home. From Monday through Friday, when we were there, they were present. They stopped in on the way to class, from class, en route to lunch, or whenever they had a free moment. They came to share news, to check on us, or to see who was already there. When they were not present they were calling with thoughts to share or questions to ask. Their questions included the date of my birthday. Lyn supplied the date and they were off and running.

In 1998 I celebrated my 49th birthday, and those five planned a surprise for the occasion. They worked with the Student Affairs Office to secure a space and persuaded the Assistant Director to get me to the room under some false premise. Normally, I am big on surprises—for others. They pulled it off with style and I knew I was loved. For the next three years, they managed to surprise me by not following the calendar and altering the setting. One year in the middle of the praise service, a week before the actual date, the entire fellowship began singing to me even as a cafeteria worker was walking in with a cake. I cried!

The students continued to shower me and each other with affection by having these small parties of love. We had become family for each other. Perhaps, upon reflection, it was somewhat superficial, but it felt authentic and it was good! Now if they would only continue to demonstrate these acts of kindness to others as they travel in this broad universe, the world would be a better place.

CHAPTER 4

Hospitality: An Ecumenical Experience

Ecumenicalism, for me, is the practice of Christianity without a particular denominational flavor. In 1989, the United Methodist and Presbyterian Churches founded the ministry as the Wesley-Westminster Campus Ministry. However, at VSU, the majority of students were of neither denomination. Our surveys have consistently shown that of students with a denominational affiliation, the majority claims the Baptist denomination. As a former Baptist, I was determined to find a healthy, informed expression that we all could embrace and appreciate. In addition, I felt a non-denominational approach was required in order to bring the local churches on board. I was correct in that assumption and received board approval to change the name to United Campus Ministry. We hoped the new name was theologically neutral and would not hinder our foray into the local church community for prayers, affirmation and monetary support. Yet, while that has allowed us to gain local church support, our biggest supporters have remained the founding partners. I am under a Methodist appointment, which means they are responsible for my salary package. However, the Presbyterians have supplied programmatic, collegial, and academic support and nurture as this practice of ministry has unfolded.

The Presbyterian Church (USA)

Functioning through the Synod of the Mid-Atlantic and the Presbytery of the James, program funds have continually flowed to us. In addition, a Campus Ministry Association is in place to offer fellowship and support for each other. They convene gatherings biannually and have consistently encouraged me to share in these gatherings. At the summer meeting, we share our highs and lows of the year, learning from each other. At the fall gathering we conduct the business of the association and share in relevant and challenging workshops. Often, opportunities for enhancement are available as well. One such opportunity, as a result of attending these gatherings, was my appointment to a task force to study the relationship of higher education and Campus Ministry.

Robert E. (Bob) Turner serves as Associate, Higher Education Ministries and Students' Ministries in the National Ministries Division of the Presbyterian Church (USA), Louisville, KY. After engaging me in numerous conversations over a two or three year period, Bob asked me to serve on this national task force.[6]

This eleven-member, diverse team would travel across the nation, viewing various models of ministry, interacting with members, and finally drafting a report of our findings as part of a recommendation for the national body. Initially, although honored, I felt unqualified to serve with this group. Nevertheless, Bob assured me that the fact I was involved in doing ministry with, for, to and by students was sufficient qualification. In fact, he added that my not being Presbyterian was also a reason he selected me, as he wanted fresh eyes. The task force included a College president, Miriam (Mim) Pride; a student, Dawn Willis; two college professors, Young Lee Hertig and Sue Lowcock-Harris; a Chaplin, Drew Henderson; Roger Dermody, a church staff member with Campus Ministry as a part of his job description; a Campus Minister; a consultant, Ed Brenegar; and Bob. Over a period of 18 months, we traveled to Louisville, Florida, California, and back to Louisville to prepare our first draft.

The models we reviewed for ministry covered a wide array. However, the two common illustrations were of parish-based

---

[6] *Renewing The Commitment: A Church-wide Mission Strategy for Ministry in Higher Education by the Presbyterian Church (U. S.A.)* This document is available at http://horeb.pcusa.org/highered/ and provides an insightful glimpse at ministry with, for, to, and by students at Ministries sponsored in part or totally by the Presbyterian Church in 1999-2001.

ministries. The students were brought to the local church and denominational ministry or a particular denomination that owned a facility on or near Campus. Students were invited to walk with them. An example of particular interest to this writer was the occurrence where two or more denominations jointly shared a building while partnering in ministry. The styles of ministry were also different and exciting to this observer.

We observed charismatic Presbyterians doing ministry in Southern California while a fundamentalist organization without a church connection, was actively engaged a few doors away. Both had more people than I did but did not appear to compete with each other. There was no prescribed way of doing this task called ministry. Each person and setting had its own set of dictates and people were responding to what they believed was right for them. Of course, I had some judgments but I held them in abeyance, too fascinated by the experience and the opportunity to learn. My options were being enlarged and my visions for ministry were being broadened. The nurturing atmosphere felt good and hospitable. They had made space for me and our ministry would be better because of their willingness to include me in the process.

On the other hand, I also observed that although there were vibrant ministries, there were many who had walked away from the church with no proclivity to be a part of the organized ministries on campuses. What does this say about this generation? What does it say about those participating in ministry at these locations?

Perhaps one lesson I learned was the absolute necessity to continuously review what we are doing. Are we as inclusive to others who appear to be different? Are we consciously engaging those on the periphery? That is, those who appear to be ostracized by their peers or who listen to a different drummer. For example, on every campus, we saw persons who appeared to have their own fellowship based upon sexual orientation. How long will we, as representatives of the church, deny these persons their full status as children of God? In addition, I watched those with visible multiple body piercings shunned as if they were an anathema. What does this say about our sense of the norm? Are we subconsciously separating ourselves based on the outward appearance of others? How does this differ from overt racial segregation?

James Daniely

Our call is to witness the name of Jesus in an environment of welcome or hostility, and at times to bring a disruptive voice to the principalities and power of this earth. What happens when we compromise our voice because of personal biases? Are we any different than the society that we are called to transform? No, we are not different; we are complacent. We allow stigmas, perceptions and ignorance to hinder the unfolding of the kingdom of God. Am I any different? What is lacking in me as a person and as a child of God involved in ministry? As I pondered that question, I enrolled in a Doctor of Ministry program at Union-PSCE. What will I find through the coursework to enrich my being? After being out of school for so many years, will I find the experience beyond me? As the only African American in the program, will my perceptions be honored? Are there persons who will pre-judge my capabilities and therefore, my work? All of these questions were vivid as I began the program.

Union Theological Seminary

Equipped with a scholarship from the United Methodist Church, I began my course of study in August of 1999. Immediately, I felt at home. The credentials of the persons attending the initial seminar were not questioned. We all came from different settings, schools, experiences of ministry, and with differing expectations. The group included persons who were United Methodists, Presbyterians, Baptists, and Assembly of God. Some came for validation, others for new insights or out of curiosity. What we found was an atmosphere of acceptance, challenge, and good will. Eventually, we even nurtured each other in various ways. Also, I began to understand and appreciate hospitality. Here is an early exponent of my understanding of hospitality written for Dr. Kay Huggins:

Since my appointment to this Ministry on Campus, most of what we do has evolved from something else. For example, we attempted various styles of worship with our students before settling upon our present style. We were looking for a pattern not only acceptable to them but also filled with integrity. We have tried all of the following at differing times with very mixed results: Interfaith gatherings, Faith Fairs and denominationally specific services, which included inviting local church groups to lead the worship. Graciously, things began to turn around. We were led to actively "market" ourselves to the First-year class of 1998. As a direct result of this prayerful marketing, we stumbled upon this participatory, non-denominational worship service. Remarkably, we found that this model was inclusive enough that few people were offended or loudly objected. We have continued to fine tune the worship service and have formed a covenant community.

While the students would not gather for Interfaith Worship, they would gather for dinner. In this setting, I see an example of Christ among the people sharing Himself. Ideologically, this would not fit all those gathered; yet I forecasted our mission clearly.

As I look back, that assignment deepened my discernment of what was occurring and allowed me to examine the implications. My fellow travelers who were also participating in a journey or process of self-discovery, encouraged this quest and offered critical evaluations of what I was interpreting for them. They also shared their journeys and allowed me to glean from their work as well. Each of them found biblical underscoring for my posture and one offered I Peter 4:8-11 where Peter admonishes us to "Practice hospitality ungrudgingly to one another. As each has received a gift, employ it for one another, as good stewards of God's varied grace: whoever speaks, as one who utters oracles of God; whoever renders service, as one who renders it by the strength that God supplies; ..." (RSV)

This is the biblical component of what I hoped was occurring on a regular basis. I was encouraging the students to be Christ to each other, and to some extent, I felt this was happening. The relationships being formed were, hopefully, reflective of a love for the other. They willingly brought their gifts of service to the ministry and shared openly. I was trying desperately to proclaim God's word as an oracle from God, at least to the best of my qualifications! The scripture seemed to be alive for us and in us.

As I sift this process further, Union, in effect, became my laboratory for refining what I was experiencing in many ways.

It was a movement or perhaps a synthesis of ideas toward this present expression of faith. However, that should not be understood as the final word. The process is still being uncovered.

In terms of my personal definition, I believe each of my professors added to my conceptual formulation through the required reading/reflections, their critique of what I shared, and their encouragement to ask myself questions and to be persistent. The union of ideas, understandings and perceptions allowed for a fresh insight of what is possible for that moment. Still, I was uncertain of where I would take this and needed guidance. Dr. Kay Huggins was especially kind in her note to me that I was using sacramental language, that hospitality is being viewed as a sacrament and as a means of grace. Until she pointed that out for me, I had intuitively understood it, but never voiced it specifically. Once that occurred, everything else fell in place. Everything I wrote about was pointing at hospitality, or was underlining and strengthening it. The Holy Spirit had allowed us to look into the practices of ministry and had sealed it. Yet, when it was time to write this project, Dr. Sam Roberts had to remind me of what I had been writing about. He had to bring me back home!

While this composition looks primarily at the ministry as it developed, what is of equal importance is my own personal development, which cannot be quantified. My experience at Union was shaping not only the ministry but also adding definition to the person I was becoming. Some understandings were being re-shaped, becoming whole. I was adding new information, which had to be processed for inclusion in the storehouse for future discernment. There is no way to adequately measure the changes in nuances of my personality. For example, no longer was uncertainty a part of my outlook. It has not been replaced with certitude, but with a quiet confidence that I knew a little more about what I was doing. The critique has sharpened the tools that the Creator grafted into my being and the experiences have caused us to grow stronger.

Furthermore, there is no way to discern when I began listening differently to the students. However, I have noticed that my listening posture, which I thought was very sensitive, is different; not better, but different. Their words have not changed, but the way I hear them has changed. Somewhere along this journey, I started being less of a fixer and started becoming a better listener to the issues being raised before me. I began to hear the hurt without searching for the cure to the problem. I was still empathetic and caring but I was not the solution, nor did I have to have the solution to the matter. At some point I was able to separate my issues from theirs and minimized the projecting. I wish I could say emphatically that I never project my issues, but that would be untrue. What I can say definitively however is that the occurrence is much less than before.

What has become of utmost importance is the willingness to just be with them. The late Dr. Miles Jones used to say, "Sometimes we just be. No answers. No quick fixes to deep matters. All we can do is just be." I think I finally understand what he was sharing more than 18 years ago. In those moments together, person-to-person, being to being, we are open to and dependent upon the Spirit. We are more than our hurts and our past; though they help to define who we are, they are not the totality of our being. We are more than the sum of our experiences. If we just allow the moment to unfold, the Spirit will provide resolution to those things that would destroy us; not necessarily the destruction of the physical body, but the destruction of the creative process at work in us at that moment. It is my prayer that I have not misinterpreted or misapplied what he was sharing. In fact, I hope that this is an accurate description of the time spent with students: sitting, praying, even hurting together, but also allowing the moment to unfold with the Creator at the center. Hence, we journeyed together to a space none of us could have predicted. Faith took us to a space called hospitality, where the Spirit embraced us and allowed us to be. Now the hope is that we duplicate that space for others, wherever we journey.

Bibliography of Suggested Books

Cooper-Lewter, Nicholas C., and Henry H. Mitchell. Soul Theology: The Heart of American Black Culture. New York: Harper & Row, 1986.

Douglas, Kelly Brown. Sexuality and the Black Church: A Womanist Perspective. Maryknoll, New York: Orbis Books, 1999.

Helminiak, Daniel A. What the Bible Really Says About Homosexuality. San Francisco: Alamo Square Press, 1994.

Howe, Leroy T. The Image of God: A Theology for Pastoral Care & Counseling. Nashville: Abingdon Press, 1995.

Loder, James E. The Logic of the Spirit: Human Development in the Theological Perspective. San Francisco: Jossey-Bass Publishers, 1998.

Proctor, Samuel D. The Substance of Things Hoped For: A Memoir of African-American Faith. New York: G. P. Putnam's Sons, 1995.

Roberts, Samuel K. African American Christian Ethics. Cleveland: Pilgrim Press, 2001.

CONCLUSION

At the outset of this reflection upon a local and specific ministry, I exercised caution regarding the portability of this model. I was, and still am, convinced that the model is transferable to other campuses within the Black experience. Especially for those involved in ministry on a Black Campus, I assure you that hospitality is more important than programs. The students must feel you are welcoming them and sense that you care for them before you can teach anything. They must feel your sacred space is also a safe space for them.

I am now convinced that this model is transferable to any campus. However, I sense a need to highlight the strengths of this effort, as well as the drawbacks to this model. Therefore, I will share the reasons for these assumptions and project a possible future for this ministry as it continues to evolve.

The components to any successful venture sometimes can be difficult to clearly define. However, in this instance, I think some of the elements are so obvious that they jump off the pages. At the outset, I must mention the given in the equation: God is involved in the process and is at the center of the interactions.

Hebrews 11:1 reads as follows: "What is faith? It is the confident assurance that what we hope for is going to happen. It is the evidence of things we cannot yet see" (New Living Translation). It is my belief that the starting point began with this faith in God and hope as articulated by Mrs. Vickie Adams. Without it, there would be no ministry at VSU. Therefore, the first building blocks in this venture were the prayers of faithful individuals believing that God would in fact honor the desires of their hearts. Perhaps this is basic, but it bears mentioning because we can sometimes overlook the rudimentary things when searching for the perceived deep things. In this instance, this step is both. The faith of Mrs. Adams and those who gathered with her was the essence of things hoped for and the evidence of things not yet seen. They believed and worked to see their beliefs come to fruition. James says: "So you see, it isn't enough just to have faith. Faith that doesn't show itself by good deeds is no faith at all—it is dead and useless" (New Living Translation). Every setting needs faithful warriors who won't just pray but will also work to see the outcome. We had a plethora of such warriors and you will also need them. They need not be on your board, but you need them like "a deer pants at the water brook."

Secondly, you need committed board members who value the ministry and are willing to take the initiative to secure its foundation. Campus Ministry, though an isolated task at times, is not a one-person venture regardless of the gifts and grace of the individual. It is a team effort. Each member of the board must share the same vision and recognize their role in getting it done. They must not be afraid to be dreamers, promoters or even correctives. They must question what is happening, why it is happening, and determine the desired outcome. They are the advisors and occasional supervisors of the Campus Minister, all vital roles. The story is told:

A little girl sees her mother cutting the wings off a chicken she is about to roast. When the little girl asks why, the mother says, "Because that's the way my momma did it." So the girl asks her grandmother, who answers, "Because that's the way my momma always did it." Finally, the girl asks her great grandmother, who says, "Because my pan was too small."

This story suggests, among other things, that we can follow examples without understanding the "why" of what we are doing. We must always understand the why of what is occurring and determine if that response is indicative of our desires. Following old patterns just because that's what we have always done will ultimately lead to complacency. We must not allow ourselves to become complacent but must continuously evaluate what, why and how we are involved in ministry. Every setting needs a board that is involved with the ministry and is willing to be supportive, financially and otherwise, but that is also willing to question what is occurring.

A third ingredient in this pie is a group of students willing to follow leadership and later assume the leadership roles. I cannot emphasize this component enough. The minister and the board must initially lead, provide learning opportunities for leadership development, take a step back to allow the student leaders to be in the lead, and finally to connect the two together. I am not abdicating that either assume all of the leadership roles, but am suggesting a shared reality. Our initial group fit this description very well but the next cycle of students has been lacking in this particular area. I am told by long-time Campus Ministers, that this is a cyclical pattern. Even if that is the case, the process must still unfold and the model must be nurtured. Even with this down cycle, leaders have been called forth; perhaps not as many as I would like, but they are present. So, while there is never a moment without student leaders, I am suggesting that their visible presence and input is imperative. Their ownership of the ministry is necessary and a desired outcome. This is a desired component of every setting as well.

The final component or ingredient in our pie is the person out front, the Campus Minister. It is absolutely necessary that he/she be committed to that role. The task tends to be at various times and seasons a solitary one. It behooves the person to be goal-oriented but not numbers driven. By that I mean to never validate success or perceived lack of success by how many people attend events. Numbers are nice, but they don't tell the whole story. Those in attendance are only the visible community; there is also the peripheral community that we cannot account for. There are staff, administrators, and other students who are impacted by what you do. Some will tell you, others will not. But remember that the One, who called you, asks only that you are faithful.

Another key for that person is to have a degree of patience, especially if they are new to the task. When you put the pie in the oven, you must wait and allow it adequate time to bake. In other words, a ministry needs time to evolve. I think five years is a good measure for a new ministry. In a paraphrase of Ecclesiastes 9:11, "The race is not given to the swift, nor to the strong, but to him (or her) that endures unto the end." To me, that implies endurance as a greater necessity than new insights or creativity, or even strength of personality. I am suggesting that time is required to adequately understand the setting, which includes identifying local support, judicatory support, local peculiarities, and discerning what God is doing at this place, and at this time. Time will also allow you to know if this is the correct fit for you. Without adequate time to allow all of these issues to surface and be brought to some resolution, I believe we can miss the mark. I believe this is a universal component of ministry regardless of setting and is therefore transferable.

A drawback to our model of ministry is the lack of a permanent facility. Yet because of a very cooperative spirit within Student Affairs, we had almost an unlimited access to the spaces we needed. With that understanding in mind, we worked to that strength and limited the types of offerings due to this missing link. Until recently, I was not convinced of the necessity of having a building, so it was not high on my agenda. However, after sharing in a leadership retreat with another ministry, I heard the concern in a new way and became very sensitive to the matter. Then to crystallize the matter, I noticed the continued occurrence of non-religious activities being scheduled in the Chapel, one even during a time-frame historically reserved for us. The student leaders were irate because their sacred space was, to them, being violated without their consultation. There is now a person scheduling the use of the building "who knew not Joseph." Will this continue to occur or was this simply an oversight? Only time will tell. But our sensitivity to the issue of space is heightened and our perceived sacred space is now not universally viewed as such. Let's examine two possibilities: our own building and shared space with a local congregation.

The cost of a building is tremendous! If we are talking about new construction (on a state campus that's the only option), the politics of getting a nearby site, zoning approval and fund raising would be Herculean obstacles. And even if we were able to overcome those matters and secure the building, we would have to maintain, insure, furnish it, etc. Some Wesley Foundations, for example, have included apartments in their building in order to provide additional income, which allows for the facility to pay for itself. Others depend on their denomination to provide most (if not all) of the costs. I will not advocate for or against having your own space. I see the advantages but also recognize that for this community it is not a viable option at this time.

What is desirable in this context is the joint use of space between a local congregation and the Campus Ministry. There is a congregation about a block away that is warming up to the idea and we are going forth slowly with our joint vision. In an ideal world, a facility a block away from campus, which meets our needs for specific programmatic concerns, would have been embraced many years ago. In the real world, age-old perceptions must be gradually erased and carefully replaced with new ideas that celebrate diversity. This is a gentle dance of the Spirit and the outcome is not yet certain. But if it becomes a reality, we want to offer Monday, Thursday, and Friday evening alternatives for the students of Campus Ministry initially, and later to the general student body. These offerings might include a seminar/dinner night, movie night or even a game night. We want all of the amenities this generation has come to expect for all to share. The wish list includes a large screen TV, video games, multiple use tables, and comfortable chairs and sofas. In formulating a covenant community, we must be intentional about finding ways to celebrate coming together, but also make it welcoming. It is our hope that our gatherings are characteristic of a loving environment and that the students and congregants will enjoy being with each other. I have not seen this specific model anywhere, but I am certain that it exists somewhere. Prayerfully, after these many years of existing without major interactions we hope now we can co-exist in the same space. Any time people of faith embrace each other it is a good thing, and it is achievable in a variety of places.

BIBLIOGRAPHY

Ammerman, Nancy et. al. Studying Congregations: A New Handbook. Nashville: Abingdon, 1998.

Chapman, Mark L. Christianity on Trial: African-American Religious Thought Before and After Black Power. Maryknoll, New York: Orbis Books, 1996.

Cone, James H. Martin and Malcolm and America: A Dream or a Nightmare. Maryknoll, New York: Orbis Books, 1991.

Lathrop, Gordon W. Holy Things: A Liturgical Theology. Minneapolis: Fortress Press, 1998.

Thomas, Frank A. They Like To Never Quit Praisin' God: The Role of Celebration in Preaching. Cleveland: United Church Press, 1997.

Thomas, Marjorie J. Soul Feast: An Invitation to the Christian Spiritual Life. Louisville: Westminster John Knox Press, 1995.

Thurman, Howard. Deep Is The Hunger: Meditations for Apostles of Sensitiveness. Richmond, IN.: Friends United Press, 1990.

Whitehead, James D. and Evelyn Eaton Whitehead. Method in Ministry: Theological Reflection and Christian Ministry. Rev.ed. Franklin, WI. Sheed and Ward, 1995.

EPILOGUE

HOSPITALITY: An International Experience

Bd. Member (A. Maven) with students

As I finalize this work, there is another aspect of our journey together that I must share. In some respects, it is the culmination of hospitality as I understand it. In May of 2002 I traveled to Gambia, West Africa with five graduating seniors: Sarah Bagley, Rebecca Gray, Damany "Smiley" Mayfield, M.

Anita Page, and Oluwatosin "Tosin" Sokoya, a board member, Ms. Carmencita Stewart, and my elder brother, Mr. Hubert Daniely, Jr. This is of major significance because these were the students who were the leaders of our ministry and who initially mentioned the possibility. Therefore, traveling outside of the continental United States was a major accomplishment for our ministry, and the hospitality that greeted us was awe-inspiring. But first, please allow me to back up and start from the beginning of this saga.

In the fall of 2001, after the devastating attack on America, my friend Musa Dampha called me from the Gambia to express his great outrage at what had occurred and to assure me that not all Moslems were joyous over the loss of innocent lives. Musa was a graduate of Virginia State University (1998) and although a Moslem had been adopted by our ministry. He was on a fellowship to study agriculture and brought his wife and youngest son with him. We became very close during his stay and maintained contact after he left. Upon his departure in 1999, he extended an invitation to visit him whenever the opportunity presented itself.

Now, three years later, the offer came again. I did not think it was possible, but I did write a grant proposal to get as close as I thought possible: Ghana. Instead, in December I received a letter and a check from the Synod of the Mid-Atlantic to travel to the Gambia. I was floored because the Gambia was where I really wanted to go! Was somebody reading my mind?

I began to plan immediately by calling my students and sharing our good fortune. They were apprehensive, but did not say no. Then I contacted members of our board to share the great opportunity and petition for a volunteer to accompany us. Ms. Carmencita Stewart, our treasurer, jumped at the idea. Because of prior travels, she knew a travel agency in Connecticut who could walk me through all the requirements! Then I contacted Musa and told him the wonderful news.

When school began in January, the talk at the office was about the Gambia and how we were going to afford to get there. We wanted to keep the traveling party small for convenience and to be able to solicit funding from everywhere! Our ecumenical partners came on board early; no one wanted to be left out once the Presbyterians had already given us several thousand dollars. We garnered the support of several local congregations and we supplemented that with fund-raising. It was coming together quickly and when May arrived, we were ready.

Two weeks after receiving their undergraduate degrees, these five students were about to embark on the journey of their lives. None had ever been out of the country and several had never been on an airplane. Yet, they had learned to trust me and we were off.

BWI Airport: Members of our group with Sarah's parents before checking in. Damany was across the lobby after his connection flight from Charlotte.

As we were awaiting our departure, I noticed the flight crew walking our way. They stood tall and walked briskly and confidently toward our gate. Others were in the airport going to differing parts of Africa, but our crew eschewed confidence and I pointed them out to my students. In so doing, I asked why did they appear so confident to them. One answered, "Because no one ever told them they could not do it!" Several in our group were flying for the first time and I saw a smile envelop their faces. It was going to be all right!

After an eight-hour flight, we arrived in Banjul, Gambia and the magnitude of the journey began to overwhelm a few; I could see it in their faces. Their countenance rose when they heard someone with a British accent screaming my name. They knew our host had arrived and we would get to leave the airport. Our luggage was brought to us and we stepped into the "Motherland." Immediately I could see that my party was tremendously disappointed with the view and several gave me a very strange look. We all boarded taxis and were off to our destination. This momentary separation, if only by a few car lengths, was unnerving for some; but we settled in the mode of things.

Our first stop was not our hotel, but to our host's home. His wife, Jamai, had prepared a feast for us. Because we were hungry, we did not complain although we were extremely exhausted. Our menu included eggs, pancakes, rice, fish, and chicken. While we were eating we were introduced again to our drivers, who ate with us and informed us they were all relatives. Musa had influenced them to take time off from work so we would be with persons he knew. Then the neighbors came into the yard to introduce themselves. En route to the residence, people waved at us and we heard choruses of "Welcome home," which made us suspicious and at ease simultaneously. This would be repeated throughout our stay in Gambia.

After eating to our satisfaction we loaded up again to travel to our quarters. First stop was the compound where the students were being housed. It was beautiful with flowery trees everywhere, banana trees along the wall and a roof entrance that allowed for a view of the neighborhood. The temperature was about 72 degrees and there was always a cool breeze. At this point the party would separate, with Hubert and me going on to another stop.

Musa's brother, Mamo, operated two hotels: the place we were leaving and Abis Bar & Restaurant, where Hubert and I would be staying. This location was a block away from the ocean and made the rest of the group jealous; but it had a nightclub immediately behind it and Musa thought it best that the young adults not be tempted constantly in their stay. Hubert and I were happy because we thought we would be away from the group. But before the day was over, our location was discovered and several of the students walked to our location looking for the beach. Along the way, they attracted an escort of several young men curious about Americans walking alone. Two industrious souls even brought their ponies along as an offer of transportation along the water.

Something in me kept saying, "Relax, you are finally home." For the first time in my existence, I did feel like I was home. All authority figures were black, all the merchants and all the people I saw that first day looked like me and I was very comfortable. It was not until the next day that I realized that Europeans also knew about this place and patronized it frequently.

That evening as we ate our dinner I reminded the group that some of the customs of our hosts were somewhat different than ours. Not better or inferior; just different, and I wanted them to acknowledge and respect them. Later, I had a private gathering with the students to ask them to journalize their visit and to seek permission before taking photographs of anyone. They agreed to comply with my wishes and later were rewarded by their personal reflections. (I wanted to include them in this work but did not get written permission to do so!)

Day two was spent acquainting us with the private schools I had written prior to our arrival. There are two Catholic schools, St. Joseph and St. Theresa, which we were working with during our visit. The former is a secondary school for young ladies and the latter a primary school for both sexes. The primary school was designated as the place where we would be most welcome.

Our next stop was at the fish market, and it was both surprising and hilarious for some. Surprising, as many of the fish on sale were familiar to those of us who loved fish. The fishermen had been out since late night and the catch was excellent. The stop was hilarious because I was startled by being handed an eel and dropped it, thinking it was a snake. My brother laughed for the rest of the day, it seems. But we had fresh fish for lunch along with broiled chicken, squash and rice (Jamai cooked again). I brought some cheeses with me and planned to have macaroni and cheese with our dinner. After dining sufficiently, we planned our excursion into the inner country. But first, we had to visit the capital city, Banjul.

The British colonized Gambia in the 15th Century and many of their customs are still observed. One such observance is maintaining a refuge for wildlife. This also served as a prelude to the trek into the heart of the nation. Gambia is a long, narrow nation that is bounded by the Atlantic Ocean on the West, the Gambian River on the North, and Senegal on the other two sides. Away from the ocean, the humidity and the heat index rose.

Banjul sits on the ocean and is a beautiful city of approximately 100,000 people. Many ethnic groups from over the breath of West Africa have flocked there, giving the city a uniqueness of its own. Many languages can be detected and Musa was fluent in many of them. As he introduced us around, faces beamed as they recognized their American brothers. (The ladies are not addressed directly.) In addition to the Gambian Museum we visited with many artisans busy pursuing their crafts and an open-air market filled with all the wonders I could have imagined.

Perhaps it was at the market that I felt most at home. There were no persons following us around as if we were suspected shoplifters. All the vendors greeted us warmly and respectfully. In fact, in some instances, they vied for our business by bringing products from behind the counters so that we could better inspect them. Yet, they respected the word "no". Although the nation is poor by western standards, crime is extremely rare and the people are carefree. Bartering is the standard means of negotiating prices and I became adept at this in short order. There were many times that I simply stepped away from our group and followed at a distance to see if I would be treated any differently than while with the traveling party. To my amazement and delight, the same warmth and friendliness was displayed and I settled in this confirmation. The remainder of our time in Gambia simply reinforced my convictions that I had indeed come home. (While in Charleston, S.C., several years later, a tour guide shared with Hubert and I that slaves were imported specifically from that region of Africa to the Charleston area to grow rice during the 16th Century. This is significant because our family descends from that area of Carolina. Could the people of Gambia possibly know this and were making the necessary connection? Probably not, but what if they did?)

The wildlife preserve was of particular interest to the students because it gave them an opportunity to view what they assumed was the natural view of Gambia. Walking along a path perhaps two feet wide, they could imagine that they were the first explorers to see this beautiful country. Monkeys played in nearby trees, oblivious to our passing. Magnificent birds flew overhead and strange, yet wonderful sounds pierced our awareness. In the middle of the preserve, behind double fences, we were amazed at the size of the hyenas, the grace of the lions and the beauty of the cranes.

Damany, Rebecca, Anita, Tosin, Sarah and Lamin
(Musa's oldest son) at the wild life refuge.

A secondary purpose of this trip was to acclimate us to the warmth away from the ocean. Over the next several days we would be traveling into the interior and the weather pattern would be different. Our paradise was dislodged by the reality of our proximity to the equator. We arrived prior to the rainy season and the prevailing winds still came from the ocean. Soon, the pattern would change and although the rain would descend from the west, the Sahara Winds would dominate the weather. It is my hope to visit during the rainy season to sample the difference.

For the students, in my opinion, the most satisfying days were the ones spent at St. Theresa Primary School. The Head-mistress, Mrs. Marie Sylva, and her deputy Mr. Gomez, permitted us the opportunity to participate in their classrooms and interact with their students. From preschool through grade six, they facilitate instruction for more than 3,000 students in two shifts. The morning session begins at 8:00 am and ends at

2:00 pm; then an afternoon session for another group of students begins at 2:00 pm and runs until 6:00 pm. This latter group also has Saturday classes. I understand there is a waiting list to be admitted. The amazing thing was not the two shifts but the scope of material covered.

We observed students being instructed in English, math, social studies, geography, science, and Aramaic, with provisions for Imams to come and instruct students in Islam. Those who were Catholic were allowed to leave and go next door to the church to receive their religious instruction. We found it most refreshing that in a Moslem nation there was no issue over students receiving instruction from other religions. In all probability because the Catholic Church had initiated this laboratory, this was viewed as healthy and was not subject to review by outside authorities. Whatever the reasoning, perhaps we in America could glean from this observation that teaching religion can be a positive tool and does not necessarily violate the rights of others. Yet, their system had some problems as well. The most obvious was a lack of technology and sufficient supplies for all the students. One student, Rebecca, tearfully observed that the writing tablets were old and in need of replacement.

At her urging, we looked carefully at the writing tablets in use and found that many of the tablets had been in service for several years due to limited resources. While we could not address their technological issues, we did think that we could supplement the meager paper resources that were available. Therefore, I briefed Mrs. Gomez with our concern and she blessed our desire to assist the school in this matter. Appropriately, when we returned to America, we began a drive to send school supplies: primarily paper, but also pencils, pens, and other needed items back to St. Theresa. Because of the generosity of our support system in the Greater Petersburg Community, we were able to meet our goals by the fall of 2002. Due to the weight of the paper and the prohibitive cost of freight, we were not able to send all the paper at once.

Our stay in the Gambia would not have been complete without journeying into the interior of the nation. It is one thing to feel welcomed in the area normally visited by tourists, but I think it is another matter to feel that genuine embrace away from the crowds. Therefore, our host planned an excursion to Janjanbureh (Georgetown), his home village, approximately two days travel from our present location.

We were told to be ready to depart by 5:30 a.m. and we crawled out of bed to begin the wait. Africans are not clock-watchers in general and our host was no exception to the rule. The idea was to begin our travel at dusk, thereby completing the bulk of the first day's journey in the relatively cool portion of the day. However, after getting up we had to wait for our travel accommodations to materialize. Musa borrowed his uncle's Land Rover and commandeered a driver for the trip. But after the driver and vehicle arrived, Jamai, Musa's wife, wanted to prepare our breakfast and package a lunch for us. While some of us waited patiently, she scrambled eggs, prepared pancakes, and fried chicken for our lunch. Then we secured ice and a cooler to transport the chicken and bottled water.

Finally, we literally climbed into the vehicle and were off. As we left the confines of the city, the natural beauty of the countryside began to reveal itself. In addition, the reality of non-paved roads began to express itself. It was not that I had never experienced dirt roads; it was that these roads had tremendous ditches in them where the torrential rains had washed away the foundation, leaving deep trenches to maneuver around. Thank God for the Land Rover! The scenery also began to change, gradually at first but then to tremendous spreads of what appeared to be barren land. However, as we observed closer we were able to see that this was actually the farming and grazing areas where the nation's food supply originated. Occasionally we would spot an oasis, where it appeared several herds were being watered together. When I asked Musa to supplement my comprehension of what I was viewing, he indicated I was correct but that also some of those oases supported rice farming as well.

After several hours of bumping along, we experienced the call of nature. When I shared this need with Musa, he immediately told us to pull over at the next village. He departed, knocked on a door, and spoke with the young lady who answered the door. She invited us—complete strangers—to use her facilities! That's hospitality. We climbed out and were ushered into her home and into the backyard. What a shock for the ladies traveling with us. There were no rest rooms but instead an area behind the house with a hole in the ground. While we waited to take turns, the children of the house greeted us. They smiled warmly, posed for photos, and then resumed playing marbles. I walked back into the compound and was pleased to observe goats roaming in a fenced area and a working vegetable garden. (Several huts were grouped together in a semicircle, with a fence along the road and an inner area that opened to the rear of each hut and appeared to be shared by all. I learned later that sometimes this was an arrangement for family security, while at other times, this was an arrangement for a man with several wives, with each wife having her own unit for her children.)

After our rest stop, we began anew and came to our first ferry crossing. The Gambian River is a rich resource for the nation and meanders back and forth in rhythm to the road as you travel to the interior of the nation. We would cross it a number of times due to the absence of bridges.

While on the ferry, we could study the life along the riverbank, watch children at play in the water and fishermen cleaning their nets. In addition, the simplicity of life enjoyed by the Gambians was refreshing and fulfilling to this observer.

Crossing the Gambian River: (Facing the camera,
from left to right, Hubert, JD, and Musa (upper corner).

At this point Musa realized that it would be better to proceed directly to our resting place for the evening rather than try to visit one of the major historic sites in the vicinity, the Wassu Stone Circles.

So we traveled near the Baboon Island National Park and spent the night in a "hotel" compound that was reminiscent of the movie images of Africa from my childhood. The tents were built to accommodate two persons but inside were electricity and running water, complete with a shower. Outside it was like a safari setting, while inside we had the comfort of an electric fan to keep us cool. There was a restaurant on site, but Musa's younger brother lived nearby and several of us went to his home to pick up our dinner for the evening. This strategy was used because several in the group were tired of riding and this would allow them the opportunity to relax while others went to procure the meal.

By our return, it was dark and there is nothing darker than an African night. If not for the sounds of the animals in the forest and the brush that bordered the road, it would have been an eerie darkness. Yet there was no danger to us because there were no predators running loose to strike fear in our hearts. This area of Africa has many monkeys and baboons. As a matter of fact, some of the gray tailed monkeys were visible to us at dawn of the next day.

Our meal consisted of fried chicken, fried yams, beans and rice. The hotel did not object to our bringing in food to the lounge and even allowed us to utilize its microwave! They had bottled beverages for sale: Coca Cola in 10oz.bottles for 25 cents. After dinner, we sat around talking about the day's journey, perceptions of this area of Gambia and impressions of the accommodations. After about two hours of sharing we turned in for the night.

Early the next day we experienced a rarity: warm water for our showers. The hotel stores water in large towers and the heat of the sun heated the water. This was our first warm shower since our arrival and we celebrated with a song. Then we climbed into our vehicle and headed toward the Wassu Stones.

We traveled to a hilly area and immediately noticed a change in vegetation. The landscape was sparsely vegetated with what can be best described as trees the size of underbrush. Soon we came to a paved highway and our travel became much swifter. We came to a fork in the road and a sign pointed us toward our destination. We turned and were surprised to find a slave museum and the stones.

According to the brochures inside the slave museum, the British first wrote about the stones in the 16th Century. At the time they were estimated to be over five hundred years old and of unknown origin. Local custom says that the area was once considered holy ground and persons came to pray for special favors. For example, if a young wife were barren she would come to these stones and offer prayers for fertility. Legend says that her prayers were always answered in the affirmative. The stones themselves are large, circular mounds with some reaching a height of more than four feet. At first glance they appear to be petrified termite mounds; but if that's the case, why didn't other termite mounds undergo the same transformation? They are grouped in circles and some appear more prominent than others. By that I mean some are larger in circumference while others are narrow and more cylindrical. Yet, there is a definite pattern to the groupings and the number to each group is set: seven per group. When you go, place this destination in your travel guide.

At midday we left and headed toward Janjanbureh (Georgetown). The British built this city during the era of slave trade and furnished it with, among other things, a school and a church. Of particular interest to me was the fact that they provided a grid for a city. We stopped at Musa's brother's home for lunch and relaxation. While lunch was being prepared, Damany and I walked the neighborhood grid and introduced ourselves as Musa's friends from America. This is Musa's home area and everyone knew him. It seems that if he had chosen to do so he would have been elected Chief of his tribal unit, a high honor but one that would require him to stay here. Since he chose not to seek the office, his uncle by marriage was selected. (An interesting conversation erupted around lineage as he was speaking on this subject; because men are allowed more than one wife if they can afford them, interesting terms have been developed to quickly clarify some relations. For example, when identifying someone as brother-brother, the speaker is saying that they share both parents. That relationship is of greater significance than a mere brother or a sister because that indicates they only share one parent! Later, upon returning to Banjul, it was shared that Hubert and I were brother-brother, and we were looked upon differently.)

An event of great magnitude was unfolding in our midst and I want to give you as much detail as possible. It surrounds the death of a distant relative of Musa's, but it is the funeral service that followed that was very significant. Musa took several of us around to meet members of his family, including the Chief, and was informed of the loss. The funeral was scheduled for the next day and I, out of curiosity, asked if it was possible to attend. He smiled and said, "No problem." We continued meeting relatives and it appeared that most of the people in that sector were related to each other and to Musa. Not only that, but Musa was widely respected and admired because he had been to America to study. When he introduced me I was lifted up as the silent provider, the person who assisted him greatly while in America. It appeared I was walking a few inches higher as we departed that night to return to our sleeping quarters.

When we returned the following morning, we immediately sensed a difference in the air. The Community was preparing to mourn the passing of an elder and preparations were obvious. We saw ladies clothed in very lovely, bright garbs while busily preparing something. I asked the driver to get closer so I could get a better look at what was happening. When he complied, I could see that some of the ladies were grinding a sort of meal into a medium size bowl. Then it dawned on me: I had asked to attend a Moslem funeral! When I mentioned to Musa that I had not realized what I was initially asking, he only smiled and said it was okay. Now I was nervous and hoped I did not offend him and that our presence would not be offensive to the Community. He assured me that no one would complain and that we would be more than welcome.

I disembarked and walked toward the ladies. Instinctively, I showed them the camera, asking if it was okay to film the moment. They smiled and I proceeded to take several images. I was amazed at the beauty and brightness of their outfits. The colors were vividly wonderful: bright reds, glowing yellows, subdued peach, and mint green, to mention a few.

Funeral Preparations: Ladies making "Charity bread."

As we moved toward the Mosque, several in the group decided they did not want to attend a funeral. I understood, but something in me said, "Pay attention." I was obedient and watched solemnly as the men of the community began to gather. They came and one by one sat quietly outside of the Mosque. In ten to fifteen minutes it appeared all the men in the community had gathered. I watched in awe and did not dare attempt to photograph this moment out of respect for what I was feeling. When had I ever experienced a moment when an entire community gathered for a funeral? Never, was the answer. Then I remembered I had observed that businesses closed for Friday prayers, and my appreciation and respect grew for the people of Gambia. They had not forgotten who they were as a people and they had welcomed me to observe their ritual of life and death, without question or reservation. I was deeply moved by the events of that day and something in me grieved. It was a loss I could not quite articulate. (The women were on the other side of the Mosque and brought us the Charity Bread at the end of the service. However, Carmencita and Sarah sat with me and no one questioned them.)

As we went to the burial ground the moment passed and the atmosphere seemed to change. The cemetery was approximately two miles in distance and many people walked. I became aware of persons wailing as they approached the burial site and I began, for some unknown reason, to think of the Gospel of John's account of the burial of Lazarus and of the women wailing. As we reached the appointed spot I noticed that the body was wrapped carefully in a lovely garment and gently deposited into the ground. (Later, I was informed that embalming is not normally practiced in this area.) As we walked away from the gravesite, several men were busy closing the grave and the conversations appeared to be reflections on the life of the deceased. An African proverb came to mind: "As long as the name of a loved one is called, that person remains alive."

We returned to the village to have lunch and were told that, in our honor, the festival dancers would perform later that day. Damany and I walked around the grid again and met some of the costumed dancers. At street corners, where several gathered, they previewed the dance for us. It reminded me of the "Ring Shout" of South Carolina in that some of the dancers gathered in a circle and invited others, inside and out, to perform to the beat of the drum. The dancing was not related to the funeral but rather to the beginning of the rainy season due to begin shortly. From the street corners and from neighboring houses the dancers gathered until the full group had assembled. They danced in rhythmical harmony and invited us to share in the experience. A few ventured into the foray, but some felt intimidated. Of course I danced, as this was a moment of our inclusion in their customs and I was not about to pass up this opportunity. (Damany recorded wonderful footage on his movie camera and shared a copy with each of the travelers.)

The next day we began our return to Banjul with new memories and impressions. Somehow the return trip was shorter. Our time together was winding down and the group was ready to return home. Yet, my soul was grieving because I did not want to leave! There was something here that was indefinable, only sensed; but it touched a deep longing within me, and I did not want to leave. The party that Musa and his family held for us on our departure was a wonderful and touching event, an emotional parting if you will, but leaving Janjanbureh was deeper. I must return, someday, to test the theory.

As I conclude this work, I believe it is necessary to restate my initial premise: we need a safe place, a hospitable space, to restore our spiritual well being. I experienced this sense of hospitality more intimately in Gambia than ever before. What I am referring to is a feeling, one that cannot be qualified or verified. It is a feeling that is neither right nor wrong, but just what I sensed deep within my psyche. Some may read that as indifference toward America, but they would be amiss. Others may conclude that this is probably my first trip abroad and these are simply feelings associated with a new culture. But they also would be in error, for I have traveled extensively.

Did others have this exact sense of our trip? Perhaps not, but that does not invalidate my experience. What should be considered in this matter are the issues that shaped me, the encounters of my life, and even the emotional state of mind as I experienced Gambia. Since no two people view similar circumstances in exactly the same fashion, I would not expect this revelation from others in my traveling party. However, if others did experience this sense of déjà vu, I don't recall another person mentioning it. Nevertheless, that's my story and I am sticking to it!

CPSIA information can be obtained at www.ICGtesting.com
Printed in the USA
BVOW08s1534200316

441044BV00002B/98/P